DESPERATION

BRETT ARMSTRONG

*This book is dedicated to the glory of God Who brings light into
the most desperate and dark hours of our loves and without
Whom there would be no words worth writing.*

Published by Expanse Books,
an imprint of Scrivenings Press LLC
15 Lucky Lane
Morrilton, Arkansas 72110
https://ScriveningsPress.com

Printed in the United States of America

Paperback ISBN 978-1-64917-234-1

eBook ISBN 978-1-64917-235-8

Editors: Erin R. Howard and K. Banks

Illustrations and map by Eric Dotseth.

Cover design by Linda Fulkerson - www.bookmarketinggraphics.com

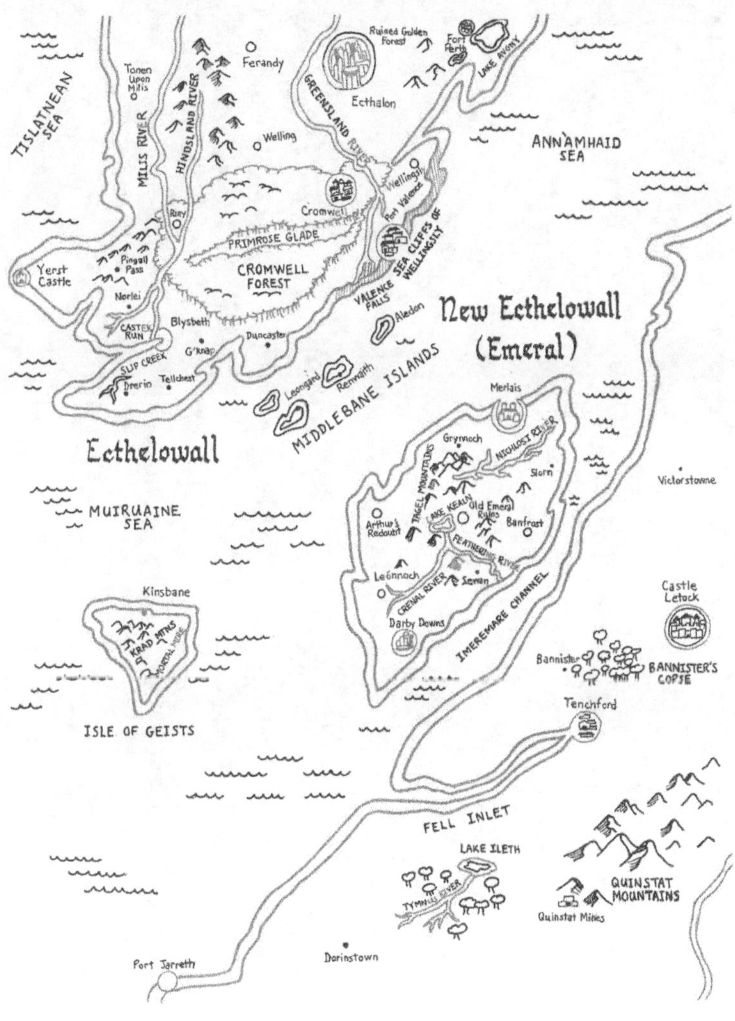

TISLATNEAN SEA
Tonen Upon Milis
Ferandy
Ruined Golden Forest
Fort Perth
LAKE AVONY
Ecthalon
ANNAMHAID SEA
MILIS RIVER
HINDSLAND RIVER
GREENSLAND RIVER
Welling
Riry
Cromwell
Wellingsli
Port Valence
PRIMROSE GLADE
SEA CLIFFS OF WELLINGSLY
Pingall Pass
CROMWELL FOREST
Yerst Castle
Norlei
Blysbeth
Duncaster
VALENCE FALLS
New Ecthelowall (Emeral)
CASTEX RUN
G'knap
Aledon
SLIP CREEK
Drerin
Tellchest
Leongard
Renvaith
MIDDLEBANE ISLANDS
Merlais
Ecthelowall
Grynnoch
NICHLOSI RIVER
Slorn
Victorstowne
MUIRUAINE SEA
TAGEL MOUNTAINS
LAKE KEALN
Old Emeral Ruins
Banfrost
Arthur's Redoubt
FEATHERING RIVER
Kinsbane
KRAD MTHS
PORTAL MORE
Leonnoch
Sevan
CREVAL RIVER
Castle Letock
Darby Downs
IMEREMARE CHANNEL
Bannister
BANNISTER'S COPSE
ISLE OF GEISTS
Tenchford
FELL INLET
LAKE ILETH
QUINSTAT MOUNTAINS
TYMNUS RIVER
Quinstat Mines
Port Jarreth
Dorinstown

ACKNOWLEDGMENTS

No book I write is ever completed without a requiring time and effort that sometimes would not be possible to take without the help of my wife, Shelly, parents Rodger and Pat, and the understanding of my day-job supervisor Andrew Neely. From them I also receive invaluable encouragement to press on and likewise am helped by all the readers who have joined me on this literary adventure. Thank you to all those whose curiosity and passion for the Lowlands have allowed me to keep exploring new lands within its bounds.

Thank you also to my publisher, Linda Fulkerson, who has immeasurable patience and understanding with my sometimes belated and wonky writerly schedules. As well as being a champion for *Quest of Fire* to the end. I'd also like to thank my editors Erin Howard and Kaci Banks for helping to hone the edge on this story and make it the most it could be.

Last and most importantly, I must acknowledge that it is wholly by God's grace and mercy I live day-by-day and without Him there would be no hope from which I could draw and none for the Lowlands either.

1

Gladiol 24, 1606 Middle Era

Hands extended, Thomas felt the soft leaves brush against his fingers. Drops of dew rolled down onto his exposed forearm, providing refreshing nips of coolness. Summer was here, and he'd been out in the sweltering heat longer than he liked. His childhood home on the Isle of Fens was far cooler, even at this time of year.

Even so, he knew better than to complain. After living five of his sixteen years with Baron Cillian Fenwrest, he learned to keep things to himself. Not that the baron, his uncle, was a tyrant. In fact, he was one of the more amenable, approachable nobles of Ecthelowall. However, no one would ever dare accuse him of being "soft." During the war with the Rehalcy to the south in which he'd lost an eye, he'd almost bled to death from his wounds. Even so, he fought an overwhelming force into full retreat. That route had earned him a place of honor on the council of nobles and been the pivotal victory of the war.

So, when it came to whining about being too hot or too

1

cold, Thomas kept quiet. And while suffocating under the weight of his boredom while guarding a noble's retinue, he kept doubly quiet.

His uncle was not here, but word would get to him. Worse, it would get to others. Baron Sornfold would be happy to see Thomas castigated yet again.

"Keep a weather eye out," a weaselly voice called out from at his back. "Never know where the Monarch's forces might strike. They're everywhere, you know?"

Thomas ground his teeth. "Of course, we're being vigilant as hawks." Above all, he repressed all complaints about Gregor. His younger cousin was his uncle's heir and well aware of it. Chubby, opinionated, and not half as smart as he imagined. It was true that Maldes Ilyron, the self-proclaimed Monarch of Ecthelowall, had spies all over the main island. Here in the southern marches, loyalty to the Viceroy was nigh universal, and there was no shortage of fervor to restore his rule. Gregor's concerns were just another of his naïve fantasies about battle. Of course, Thomas couldn't say any of this aloud.

"We should pick up the pace," Gregor added. "Her Mistress, Delia, need not suffer the heat of your sloth."

Rolling his eyes, Thomas spurred his horse on faster. "How did Uncle Cillian's son of all people become so pretentious?" he muttered under his breath.

A snicker at his left told him Sir Hurstwell heard his comment. The old man, and captain of Baron Fenwrest's guard, was the closest thing to a friend Thomas had out here. At times he felt like a well-armored nanny as much as a mentor.

Wiping sweat from his brow, Thomas cleared soaked strands of his chestnut brown hair from his eyes and glanced back. Gregor appeared none the wiser. The little oaf swatted at mosquitoes and wasn't attending to the reins of his horse. Usually, Thomas would warn him about it, but right now,

Gregor was too insufferable. Mistress Delia was his betrothed, and he acted especially pompous around her.

Delia, eldest daughter of Baron Sornfold, was eighteen with long, curly amber tresses, smooth skin bearing the faintest traces of freckles on each cheek. Her eyes were blue like the Hindsland River and intelligent. Her name meant sun-kissed, and there wasn't a man or boy in all Ecthelowall who didn't envy the sun. She was all but oblivious to Gregor. In fairness, she wasn't much interested in anyone after her first fiancé Mark, Gregor's older brother, died from a gangrenous wound received when the War of Restoration started. Twenty-one, handsome, courtly, and her true love. Whatever annoyance Gregor induced, Mark had in equal amounts awed Thomas. Mark was his hero and acted every bit like a brother instead of a cousin.

It was perhaps forgivable if Gregor presumed the respect and rewards due his brother were from title instead of virtue. He was Baron Fenwrest's youngest child; how could he understand the world's hard things? Or the need to earn respect?

There was a flicker of movement that drew Thomas's attention. Another girl, seated beside Delia, had crossed her arms over her chest. It was hard to tell from this distance, but he thought her brow arched, and a question burned in her emerald eyes.

His cheeks flushed red, and he turned back around. Mia was Thomas's age and Delia's younger sister. A thorn in Thomas's side, no doubt she was gossiping about him gawking at her sister, which wasn't true. Beautiful as she was—Thomas wasn't that disrespectful. Especially not to Mark's Delia. But from their childhood up, whenever the spiteful redhead could, she got him into trouble. Her life's mission seemed to be his misery.

"How much farther till we reach Yerst Castle?" Thomas tried not to sound flustered.

His efforts were in vain. On the rumble of a chuckle, Sir Hurstwell replied, "We've barely left Cromwell. It'll be two, maybe three days at this pace. Naught to fear, though, Master Thomas. I will protect you from Mistress Mia."

"She's not a mistress," Thomas corrected him. Everyone seemed to ignore her impertinent behavior, excusing its implicit rebellion against the social order. If Thomas had to follow it and wait hand and foot on his boor cousin, then Mia wasn't getting a pass from him.

"Well, she's certainly not a man," Hurstwell countered. "Surely you've noticed."

"What do you mean by—"

A dozen yards ahead, a figure burst out of the tree line at a sprint. The next instant Hurstwell was after him. Two seconds after, Thomas flanked him.

The man ran perpendicular to travelers. It took them nearly running him down for him to even notice their pursuit.

As soon as they had him flanked, he threw up his hands. "Please, I only want to warn my family! Please, sir. They're just a little farther in Duncaster."

"And that blood on you, that's yours alone?" Hurstwell asked, sounding as though he doubted it very much.

Thomas looked the stranger over as the man dithered answering. Hurstwell's question was fair. The man's garments were streaked with a rich crimson. They looked like the undergarments of a soldier over a common woodsman.

"It's not mine. Not most of it anyway," the man grew quiet, holding out his shirt from his body to examine it. There was a change as he did. His thready calm broke and his eyes widened as tremors seized him. "You have to run! They're coming!" he shouted and tried to sneak from between Thomas and Hurstwell.

Hurstwell snagged the man by the scruff of his collar. "We'll be needing more cause for flight in the free country of Ecthelowall than that, I'm afraid."

"But this isn't free land anymore," the man protested. "The Monarch's forces are coming!"

"The Monarch's armies were pushed back north of the Greenstrand River's bend," Hurstwell pointed out, shooting Thomas a look that said they were dealing with a lunatic.

Shaking his head, the terrified man held up his hands. "Please, sirs, I want no trouble. I am a deserter, I admit that. But if you'd seen what I had, you'd have run too."

"And what exactly did you see?"

"An unbelievable force. An army three times as large as the Monarch's levies attacked us by surprise at dawn. In the Primrose Glade, north of here. I was lucky to survive."

Hurstwell spat. "When the Viceroy's armies arrive—"

The deserter stopped struggling to free himself. A sound, which began as a laugh but perished as a moan, escaped his mouth. "You don't understand. They're gone. All of them. There is no army left. There is no Viceroy. We're all going to die."

Thomas blinked and looked over at Sir Hurstwell, aghast. The War of Restoration turned in their favor not two months earlier with the arrival of Albaron's soldiers in the north. This man had to be exaggerating. What mortal army of the Lowlands could assemble and devastate the strong alliance the Viceroy had here in the Cromwell March?

"You have to make him bring us there!" Mia demanded, her eyes fierce. "Delia, tell them! Father was encamped there."

"Yes, but it's a battle. We could get hurt!" Gregor protested, looking panicked by the very idea of seeing the battle, much less drawing into its enclosure.

"Oh, grow a spine," Mia sniped.

"Mia!" Her sister chided. Delia's eyes fell to the ground. "I do not think that's wise, sister. Whether this man is lying or not, a place such as that is precisely where Father would not want us to be. It's better for us to stay the course to Yerst Castle." Her voice sounded hollowed out, as though she'd already resigned herself to the loss.

It tore at Thomas. He wasn't Mark, but he knew better. If he cared at all for Delia and his memories of Mark, he knew what he had to do. "I'll go."

Beside him, Sir Hurstwell grunted and shot him a wary glance. Thomas took it as a challenge. "I can do it. I'll take this deserter back to the field, and we'll sort this out. The rest of you can double back to Port Valence to be safe, and I'll join you later with news of what's happened."

Mia's lips pursed as if she wanted to say something, but Sir Hurstwell cut her off. "Too dangerous for you, young one. I'm in charge of your care as well. We all head to Valence and that's the whole of it."

"No!" Mia screeched and jumped down from the carriage, landing with surprising grace. "If you won't take us there, I'm going alone." With that, she bunched up the jade mounds of her dress and took off into the trees.

Hurstwell uttered a growl and pointed to Thomas. "Well, there you have it. Get after her. I'll guard the others and proceed on to Port Valence." He addressed the deserter, "It's a high crime to flee from battle without orders."

The man looked stricken. "Please! No! I'll die—we'll all die!"

"How far north and east are the battle lines?"

"Haven't you been listening? There are no lines. It was a massacre!"

"How far?" Hurstwell barked, his voice firm and fast as a boulder.

"Three, maybe four miles if you cut across the forest," the man used his sleeve to wipe tears from his eyes.

"Good. Now, get. If I see you again, I'll be forced to exact the due penalty from you," Hurstwell swore pointedly.

The man mumbled a thanks and then took off running. Thomas watched him until Sir Hurstwell whistled. The large man pointed to the tree line. "What are you waiting for? Get Mistress Mia."

2

Thomas had been through the forests of Cromwell March many times. He knew how to walk and run through the dense confluence of trees with speed and stealth. His footfalls, even at a sprint, were the padded tread of the hunter. Perhaps his experiences on hunts made him over-sensitive, causing him to wince at each faint crunch and rustle he created. But the impossibly loud thrashing of Mia … well, the forest itself deserved better than that. Not to mention, if the deserter spoke true, her crashing through the undergrowth was incredibly dangerous.

He gave Mia about a quarter mile to come to her senses. She didn't. Running ahead, he came around in front of her. Mia gave a startled yelp of surprise.

"A grizzly bear at a full run in a potter's shop makes less noise than you," Thomas grumbled.

Leveling a stare that could melt through steel, Mia demanded, "Get out of my way. I'm going to see my father."

"Baron Sornfold charged Hurstwell and me with keeping you safe. If he and the others in the Viceroy's army moved camp this near our route, it's not because he intends for you to be there," Thomas challenged, moving to the side as Mia tried to skirt around him.

"Ugh, you're such a pest. You and Hurstwell are like trained dogs, following every passing whim a nobleman stumbles upon!"

"No, just the ones that make sense. You know, keeping maniacs like you from getting hurt," Thomas countered, letting his voice grow as loud and forceful as hers.

There was a softening of Mia's scornful expression. After a moment, she said, "You're just looking out for me then?"

Thomas nodded. "Of course. I want to know the truth about this battle, but your safety comes first. It's my duty to get you to Yerst Castle without harm."

Mia drifted closer to him. At first, he thought it was to dodge past him, but she didn't take her eyes off his. Without any warning, she brushed her fingertips along the length of his arm so gently it sent shivers through him. Her eyelashes seemed to flutter, and her lips slightly parted. If he had to characterize it and the way she angled her bodice towards him, he came to an absurd conclusion.

"Are you trying to flirt with me right now?" he asked, completely blunt and more than a little confused.

Her hand dropped and she huffed. "Isn't it obvious? Or are you too dense to understand that either?"

He pointed at her. "That's more of what I was expecting. How dumb do you think I am that I'd just fall for you suddenly acting as though you tolerate me, much less have feelings for me?"

"Well, I see the way you drool over my sister. It wasn't such a leap to think you're that dopey. She clearly manipulates you all the time. I thought I'd give it a shot."

Thomas laughed. "Maybe, but your sister is beautiful and thoughtful and gracious."

"And I'm not?" She replied, hands on her hips, her eyes filled with a challenge.

"I—uh," he struggled. How could he compare the two of them? Though as he stared at Mia, the ferocity in her countenance did make her seem older, more mature. The more he looked, the more he could see through the angry façade to the concern and caring for her father. Cast in that light, she suddenly looked very different. Not stubborn or pigheaded, but passionate, loyal, determined. "I suppose you are beautiful in your own ways," he commented before he could catch himself.

Her cheeks flushed red. "What did you say?"

"Nothing," he said quickly and then added, "We're still at least two and a half miles from the battlefield. If you stick with me, I can help you tread quieter so we get there in one piece."

Mia cocked her head to the side, sending her ruddy curls sliding over her shoulder. "Are you serious? You're going to help now?"

"Yes, but only if we move fast," he asserted. "We'll need to see what's happened and get back to the group before they worry I've lost you."

She stared at him, thoughtfulness knitting her brows. "Okay," she finally said. "Lead the way, and I'll try to move more quietly."

MAKING it through the forest took longer than Thomas wanted. Mia, true to her word, did try. Even so, he had to go much slower and take a more winding path to ensure they weren't found. Whether the deserter told the truth or not, approaching a battlefield unexpected wasn't something to do loudly.

"There's a clearing just ahead," he informed her as he made his way up a slope of a creek bed. "From what our deserter friend told us, it makes the most sense for a battle—"

He stopped, every muscle going stiff as if caught in a trance.

"Most sense for what?" Mia pressed. She was about two yards behind him and hadn't yet struggled up the bank. Thomas kept silent and waited for her.

"Hello? Finish your sentence," she said and fumbled a bit on the slick stones.

He reached down, grabbed her wrist, and hauled her the rest of the way up. She jerked back her hand and looked ready to say something undoubtedly scathing when she caught sight of what he'd seen. Mia gasped. Most of the line of trees suddenly ended in shattered smoking stumps. Out in the glade beyond stretched bodies of fallen soldiers. Hundreds. Maybe thousands. Fires still smoldered in some spots and destroyed cannons and downed horses only added to the cataclysmic feel of the landscape.

As the shock at the desolation gave way to disgust and anxiety, Thomas scanned the field for signs of the victors. Judging from the proliferation of the Viceroy's standard and colors, the deserter had been right. This had been a slaughter.

It struck Thomas after nearly a minute of surveying the carnage that he'd heard no sounds from Mia. Facing her, he was surprised to find her not weeping hysterically or boiling with anger. Instead, she took it all in with what could best be described as solemnity.

Thomas understood the look. He'd worn it himself years before. It was that of one who, in a single moment, lost everything dear to them in the Lowlands.

3

"Mia?" he inquired, concerned she might be going into shock. "We can sit down on that tree trunk over there if you need a moment." In truth, he'd given her nearly five minutes already. As much as he felt her pain in ways she likely didn't know, they couldn't linger. They had to get back to the others.

"Mia?" he tried again and reached out and gently put his hand on her shoulder.

"No, I'm fine." She evaded his touch. "I can't believe he was right. We were still celebrating the victory that turned back the Monarch and guaranteed Cromwell's safety for good. But somehow, we've lost everything. Our safety. The Viceroy. Father. They're just gone."

"We don't know that for sure. Both the Viceroy and your father could have been in the back of the lines; maybe they escaped during a strategic withdrawal."

She shot him a glance, eyes reddened with suppressed tears. "Father doesn't retreat, and he would never let his men fight dangers he would not face himself."

Thomas looked at the ground. He did know that, and could respect the Baron for it. "Whatever our differences, your father is an honorable man."

"Was," she corrected. "Was honorable. No one else escaped this. This is the worst slaughter in Ecthelowall's history. I can see the bodies of pages and nursemaids. What kind of monster kills them?" A tear slid down her cheek, and she wiped it away, but she was breaking; a faint moan escaped her lips.

Running his hand through his hair, Thomas scanned the area. They had to hurry, but he knew he couldn't force her on. Heartbreak has a way of numbing the body to the survival instincts outward injuries excite.

He wrapped his arms around her and felt her grip him fiercely. She sobbed into his chest. Thomas rubbed her back gently, murmuring soothing sounds.

After a few moments, Mia pushed away and regarded him warily. Her voice choked as she asked, "What are you doing?"

He raised his brows. That was a delicate question. She might fall apart if he revealed his belief that her father was gone. But as he looked into her pain-stricken eyes, he recalled how he'd longed for honesty in his time of hurt. "Um, I guess I'm consoling you."

She shook her head. "We can't even stand being in the same room together. Why would you want to console me?"

Suspicion was heavy in her voice and her tone much louder now. Whatever she thought he was up to, it was clearly blinding her to the precarious position they were in. He held up his hands placatingly. "Easy. I meant you no ill. I just understand, is all."

"Understand? Understand what?"

He sighed. "What it's like to lose a father. To lose everything."

Mia blinked and looked around as if lost. Finally, her eyes returned to him. "I'm sorry," she said, her voice a little steadier. "I forgot about your ... situation. I just ... I can't ..."

Her attention was fixed on the ruined glade again. Her hand rested over her mouth as if to stifle a cry.

Taking a deep breath, Thomas scanned the field. He couldn't spot what he was looking for and stalked off through the green, calf-high grasses which swayed in the summer breeze. Places like this always seemed inordinately calm.

"Wait," Mia grabbed his arm, pulling him back. "I said I'm sorry. Where are you going?"

He didn't fight her, though his own internal rends reopened in all of this. Thomas was managing his anger better than he had in a long time. "I'm going to find your father's standard. We'll need to present it to the mayor at Port Valence. Someone in authority will have to confer his title."

"Oh," she said, sounding like she felt a fool. "That's very practical of you."

"It's the best I can do for you and your sister right now," he said with a shrug. "We'll have to hurry and get back to the others. It won't be safe for any of us out here for much longer."

Mia nodded. "You're right. I forgot about Delia. She'll be destroyed." She let go of him and gestured for him to proceed.

When he started across the field, though, she stayed close beside him. For once, he didn't feel annoyance radiating from her and found that, in its absence, his own distaste for her evaporated—just another bizarre twist to this strange and devastating day.

About fifty yards into the field, Mia called out, "Over there!" She rapped on his arm and pointed some fifteen more yards away.

Sure enough, the banner for Baron Sornfold dangled off its

pole at a shallow angle to the ground. Before he could commend Mia's find, she took off at a dash, her dress hiked to her knees.

Thomas got to it first and winced at the grisly sight. He held up a hand to get her to stop, intending to spare her. An enormous crater gaped before him. On its periphery were the scorched and mangled bodies of those who had been too near the impact. What sort of bombardier caused this, he could only guess. He had seen some examples of cannons while with his uncle. But this surpassed all of them.

Curiosity seized him, morbid and potent as when he was a young boy and had witnessed injured horses being killed after a battle. It pulled him to the edge of the crater, and he peered in.

Immediately he had to blink at what he saw. In the midst of the scorched ruin of earth was a soldier in silver plate mail. Thomas guessed the warrior must have fallen in because there were no dulling or scratches on his armor. But the crater seemed shaped around his body as if he had been crushed into the soil by the blast's force.

"What in the Lowlands?" Thomas muttered.

"What is it? Did you find my father?" Mia's voice quavered.

She hadn't listened and came right upon him and gasped. With a sigh, Thomas slunk around the crater and wrenched the standard fabric from the frame to which it was tethered. "Come on, we have what we need. Let's go."

Mia wobbled, took a bad step, and slid down into the crater, crashing into the knight's body. In a futile attempt to keep the whole thing from happening, Thomas lost his footing and came to land beside her.

"Some escort you are," she muttered and scrambled to her feet. The sharp and demeaning quality to her words that had formerly grated on Thomas's nerves was noticeably absent.

"Thanks. You know you—"

"Ugh."

"I 'ugh'? Really? What does that even mean?" Mia whirled around, looking a bit annoyed or, quizzically, dismayed. Then she noticed what had interrupted Thomas. The body on the ground was the source of the groan.

4

Instinctively, Thomas grabbed Mia by the arms and placed himself between her and the soldier. Finding his footing, he hauled them both out of the crater and led her several steps away. He spun around, trying to sort out the situation.

"Thomas?" Mia whispered to him. "What do we do?"

"I don't know. He's not wearing the colors of the Viceroy or the Monarch. Though he is near your father's banner?"

Just then, the soldier climbed out of the crater. His impressive silver armor was covered with inscriptions etched into nearly every surface of the plate mail, each one catching the light and gleaming. He favored one leg and held his head. After a few seconds of groaning, he removed his helmet. The soldier scanned the battlefield in all directions. After several seconds he turned to see Thomas and Mia watching him.

He had short light brown hair and was probably a few years older than them. His bone structure and skin tone suggested he could be from Ecthelowall, but more likely Libertias. Small green eyes examined them both before the tension relaxed in his face, and he offered a slight smile. "Hello there," he said, his voice sounding hoarse.

"Hello," Thomas replied, wary.

"I see you have a standard from one of the barons supporting the Viceroy. Can I assume you are both loyal to the Viceroy?"

"You can assume we want no trouble," Thomas replied.

The other teen cocked his head and rolled his eyes toward the field behind him. "Looks like trouble is yours nonetheless. I'm Terrillian, Knight of Light in service of the Viceroy." He held out his arm slightly tilted. It was a traditional Ecthel greeting of friends, but he did it somewhat awkwardly.

"You're from Libertias, aren't you," Mia commented. "I can tell by your accent."

Terrillian laughed. "You're quite the observer. I do come from Libertias, Black River in Walhonde County."

"I've never heard of it," Mia admitted, sounding perplexed.

"Me either," Thomas added, still trying to keep between Mia and this strange knight from another land.

"You wouldn't, likely. It's a small place. Pretty backwater, or backwoods, as we'd say." He chuckled about something.

"What brought you to Primrose Glade?" Mia asked.

Terrillian looked out at the battlefield and gestured to it. "I've been fighting alongside the Viceroy to overthrow the usurping Monarch. I guess I got knocked unconscious during the battle."

He turned his attention back to Mia and Thomas. "Judging from what I see, we didn't win, did we?"

Thomas answered, "We don't know, but a deserter from the Viceroy's army said the defeat was catastrophic, and the Viceroy's army was shattered."

Terrillian's face fell. His countenance betrayed how genuinely this news broke him. "May the High King receive them all into his Kingdom," he murmured. After a moment of silence, he nodded to Mia and Thomas. "Do you know which direction the retreat took?"

"No," Mia answered. "We were on our way to Yerst Castle when we found out the news." Pausing, she gnawed her lip and shot Thomas a glance, possibly regretting her openness. Suddenly, she blurted, "Baron Sornfold, he was here, wasn't he? Did he fall?"

Terrillian stared at her for a few moments and then shook his head. "No, um, I think I heard that the Viceroy sent him and Baron Gloarch to New Ecthelowall to begin rallying additional men from there. They left a day or more ago."

Mia put her hand to her mouth and swayed, unsteady on her feet. Thomas caught her and helped keep her steady. The drastic swing in fortunes were going to tax her. Best to get back to the others as soon as possible. To Terrillian, he commented, "We have to meet the rest of our party at Port Valence. You can come with us if you would be benefitted."

Terrillian looked up and then at the battlefield. He shook his head. "No, I don't think going to Port Valence would be a good idea. Our strongest remaining support base in the south is New Ecthelowall. If the battle went as poorly as it seems, the Monarch will no doubt move on it to cut off supplies from reaching the remnants of the army here. Presuming there are any."

Thomas glanced at Mia the same instant she turned to him. She wore a similar expression of concern. "We must get to Sir Hurstwell and your sister before they wander into a siege."

"What can we do? If we don't get to the port and set sail, we'll be trapped here. Once they know Father is out of reach, they'll come for Delia and then me. Not to mention Gregor."

Gritting his teeth, Thomas knew what she meant. His family was one of two with heraldry tracing to the last

Monarch. If the Cromwells were wiped out here, as well could be the case, Gregor could be the only legitimate rival claimant to the Monarch crown. Unlike Thomas, whose noble claims died with his parents in a castle fire. It was the first time having lost so much actually meant Thomas was better off than Gregor.

Mia pointed out, "We're all as good as dead if we stay."

"Agreed," Terrillian replied. "But I might have an alternative. Are you familiar with the Sea Dragon?"

"You mean Captain Nerebold, the privateer?" Thomas asked, unable to quell his sudden interest.

"He's a legend," Mia interjected as if trying to temper Thomas's excitement.

"Arnauld Nerebold is most definitely a real person. He helped us smuggle the Viceroy back onto the island. And his ship should be anchored about twenty miles southwest of Port Valence. If we make for there, he should be able to get us passage to New Ecthelowall."

"We have to go now if we're going to head off Sir Hurstwell and your sister," Thomas pointed out to Mia.

She looked at Terrillian for a moment and then whispered to Thomas, "Do you trust this Terrillian? This could all be a trap."

"It's a gamble we'll have to make. Trap or no trap, we don't have many options for getting through this alive other than for us to run off by ourselves."

"I would never abandon, Delia," Mia seethed.

"And I would not ask you to. See, our decision is made for us."

Scowling as if frustrated by the inescapability of it all, Mia replied, "Very well. We head off my sister and Hurstwell and then on to Captain Nerebold." Mia turned to face Terrillian. "Lead the way, Sir. But one word of caution."

"What's that?" Terrillian asked.

"Don't call Emeral 'New Ecthelowall.' The islanders are fiercely proud and independent. They don't take kindly to it."

"She ought to know," Thomas interjected. "Her mother's from there."

"Got it. Let's hope resilience is another trait they possess. Once we land, the Monarch will come, and as you can tell, he doesn't show mercy."

5

Pushing aside a bough, Thomas motioned for Mia to come forward. Terrillian was already out on the main road waiting for them, but Thomas insisted on checking before she exited the dense wood they had cut across to make up for lost time.

Mia didn't hesitate. Her dress was in tatters now, and they'd completely cut away everything below her calves to make it easier. That was the greatest sacrifice of propriety to practicality she was willing to make. As she passed by, he noticed a bit of foliage caught in her thick auburn tresses, which were in tangled disarray at this point. Not to mention the scratch on her cheek from dashing too close to a branch. Neither he nor Mia would be very convincing as members of a noble party. Not that he had ever been in his simple tunic, trousers, and vest.

Stepping out of the shade onto the sunlit road, Thomas marveled at how Terrillian's armor gleamed in the sun. The silvery plate mail reflected it as well as a mirror, though it must be comprised of something sturdier than pure silver. He knew legends of orechal alloys from Tislatna. Thomas wondered if that was what he saw now. Terrillian certainly evoked a sense of having stepped out of legends. Fit as Thomas was, Terrillian had outpaced him without becoming even slightly winded.

"This is the road your party will pass along, correct?" Terrillian asked as they walked.

"We're probably a mile ahead or behind them, depending on how fast they're traveling. Knowing Sir Hurstwell, it's the former."

Beside him, Mia stirred. "No offense, Sir Terrillian, you're not Ecthel, and given your obvious lack of mannerisms, your family hasn't been either for some time. How is it you came to be supporting the Viceroy's cause?"

Terrillian laughed. "I wouldn't have known to be offended if you hadn't told me. But as it happens, you're right. I come from a well-embedded Libertian family. I'm here because the High King directed me to be."

"And the Loyalist Nobles approved?" Mia pressed. Thomas wasn't sure what her angle was here.

Shrugging, Terrillian replied, "That I wouldn't know. Viceroy Ecthelion said he was pleased to have my aid, though."

"You know the Viceroy personally?" Mia sounded envious and suspicious in one.

"I suppose so," Terrillian answered easily, not a stutter in his stride. "We fought together in Ordumair to stop the Grey Scourge. Which is something I'd prefer to talk about another time if you don't mind."

Mia shook her head. "The Grey Scourge? The High King? You live in a world of fanciful tales, don't you?"

"Mia," Thomas chided. Not so much for Terrillian or his own disagreement as on Hurstwell's behalf. The old captain was a Palatini Lucis Aeternae, a Knight of Light, himself. The only one Thomas had ever known well enough to respect.

"It's okay," Terrillian assured. "I once had some doubts about some of it too. But I suspect you'll see the world is more wonderful and terrible than you believe by the end of this day."

"Did your king tell you that?" Mia retorted, barely veiling her snark.

"As a matter of fact, he did," Terrillian replied, his voice dread serious. He stopped and faced them both. "I was on an important quest before coming here. And no offense, but if this was just about some silly political jostling within Ecthelowall, I wouldn't have been sent here."

That said, he returned to walking and kept a faster pace than Mia and Thomas could quite manage.

"A bit self-righteous, isn't he?" Mia whispered.

"I guess it depends."

"On what?" she asked when he left it at that.

"If he's right," Thomas answered with ease and shot her a smirk.

She sighed and gave him a half-hearted shove. "You're terrible."

"Hey," he called out, irked. A more scathing comment died in his throat. There was a quiver in Mia's lip, and her eyes were wide. She was riding on adrenaline. The good turn for her father was buoying her, but the danger they were in hadn't escaped her. Thomas understood; she was coping by delving headfirst into distractions. Like picking a fight with him. "That wasn't very noblewomanly of you," Thomas settled on as reply and gave her his smarmiest grin.

"Well then, you really won't like this," she rejoined and threw all her weight into a shoulder check that sent him stumbling into the road's ditch.

He slung bits of mud off his hands and glared up at her, which she returned with equal heat until she snickered and started chuckling. "You won't be laughing when I toss you down here." The threat was apparently loud enough that Terrillian stopped to look back. Thomas thought he saw the other teen chuckling too.

"Ahhh!"

Thomas froze where he stood, half in the ditch, half out. That scream had come from just ahead, where walls of thick boughed trees on either side of the road blocked their view around a bend.

"That was Delia!" Mia took off running down the road.

"Wait!" Terrillian called as she dashed past him.

Thomas ran up beside him. "No use calling like that, she's definitely got Emeral in her."

Terrillian huffed and took off to catch up, Thomas on his heels. When they reached Mia, Terrillian ran ahead and blocked her path. She stopped and tried to slip around him, which he moved to block each way she tried.

A gale at sea has far less fury than her expression held. "What are you doing? We have to—"

"Be careful. If what you said is true, an entire army could be surrounding her."

"I won't let those beasts hurt her!"

"Right now, my concern is for you two," Terrillian replied. "We're going to try to help your sister, but we have to be smart."

Mia's scowl darkened. "Fine. Lead the way then."

The Libertian teen assessed the road in each direction and then gestured to the trees. "Let's come around from in there."

They had to be painfully slow and methodical, but at length, they were on a lower slope looking up from the concealment of the trees' undergrowth at Delia and the others. Hurstwell was unconscious on the ground, and there was a circle of soldiers around Delia and Gregor, who were both still in the carriage. Gregor's face was screwed up in terror, but Delia surveyed the scene coolly. Thomas was about to propose they rush them when one of the soldiers turned his head in their direction. Eyes wide, Thomas gaped and heard Mia gasp.

The man facing their direction looked wrong. He was too pallid, too gaunt, and too unfocused in his gaze to belong to Ecthelowall's standing army. Tiny spiderings of purplish lines were visible under his skin. Thomas didn't have a word for it. Indeed the man looked closer to a thing from a nightmare than the reality unfolding before him.

"Those can't be soldiers," Mia whispered. "But they don't exactly look like bandits either."

"As well patrolled as this road is, I wouldn't expect there to be a group of bandits this large either," Thomas added.

Terrillian huffed. "I don't like this. There's something not right about them. They feel off."

"Care to share how you 'feel' their being 'off'?" Mia questioned, her mouth quirked up in a dubious expression.

"This is how," he responded and partially drew his spiritsword from its scabbard. Heat roiled from the blade, and Thomas thought he could see a faint glow emanating. He had heard stories from Hurstwell, but this was something else entirely. In fact, the longer he watched, the more he felt sure he could see flames dancing around the exposed portion of the blade and tiny letters glowing like coals.

"Your sword? Is that it? You have an itching sword hand?" Mia derided.

"Can't you see the fire on it?" Thomas asked. Doubt struck him for just a moment, but upon taking in Terrillian's approving expression, he realized he wasn't imagining it.

Mia chuckled lightly and then stopped. "Wait, you're serious?"

"Yes, just look closer at the inscriptions."

"It isn't polite to tease," she reproved.

"This isn't a joke," he insisted. "Just try, please."

She rolled her eyes and stared at it. Her face was sullen until there were footsteps from beyond the tree line and a sudden flare raced along the sword.

Mia stumbled back, a startled squeal escaping her lips before she covered them. She stared up at Thomas, eyes wide.

He smirked back at her, but only for a second. Terrillian stood from his crouch and drew his sword fully. "They're coming," he said. "You two stay back."

As if admitted by those words, five of the strange men they were observing burst from the tree line. They seemed to blankly assess the three as one might particulates of dust drifting in sunbeams.

Then one of them tilted its head at an odd angle, and his lip curled up in a snarl. He was staring at Terrillian's sword. He let out a guttural howl and charged forward. The four others seemed to instantly snap to the offensive on his command.

They came at Terrillian in fumbling brutish attacks more characteristic of animals than people. Thomas felt bile rise in his throat, horrified and intrigued in one, and barely noticed when Mia clung to him.

Terrillian brought his sword around in a defensive display, intending to dissuade it seemed. But the first man ran straightway into the flourish, yelping as the fiery blade grazed him.

He went down to one knee, smacking at the flames, then stood and leaped at Terrillian, who whirled out of the way and slammed the pommel of his sword into the face of the man. A third landed a glancing hit on his cuirass, forcing him to make a light-footed dodge backward. "Terrillian is remarkably nimble in that armor," Thomas mumbled, half to himself, half to Mia.

Mia gave him a violent shake.

"Hey? What's the matter with you?" he grumbled before realizing she was pallid and pointing to the tree line. A dozen more had emerged. Then four more. The group all moved in unison towards Terrillian, but the four latest approached Thomas and Mia.

Thomas looked around, frantic, then shoved Mia towards the tree behind them. "Climb it. Get out of reach!"

Two seconds later, the first of them was on him, and he threw everything he had into a right hook across the man's jaw.

The man spun backward from the blow. Staggered, turned, his lower lip dripping blood and saliva—and charged right back at Thomas.

Thomas stared in disbelief. From the ache radiating in his hand, he knew that hadn't been a light blow. Dropping into a fighting stance he'd been taught by Hurstwell, he dodged the man's attempt to grab him and hammered both fists overhead onto his back, sending his off-balance attacker to the ground.

That's when the second of the quartet reached him and clubbed him over the shoulder.

Dropping to one knee, Thomas turned around just in time to be seized and violently thrown against the protruding roots of the sweet gum tree they were under. For a brief moment, as he sucked in a sharp breath and clutched at his aching abdomen, he saw a blur whirling through the midst of the mass of attackers. By now, nearly the whole group had come down against Terrillian.

That was all Thomas saw before a sharp kick to his back followed by another to his belly and legs forced him to curl into a ball. Scratches, punches, and kicks rained down on him as the vacant-eyed fiends assaulted him from all directions. Curling as tight as he could manage, he braced himself and hoped fervently for rescue. Everything was pain and blood. His vision went blurry, and he blacked out, knowing this was the end.

6

"Thomas! Thomas!" Mia's fervent cries pierced the dark, numb space his mind retreated to and pulled him back to consciousness as though surfacing from a deep dive in Lake Avony.

His eyes fluttered open, and it took a moment to focus them. Mia loomed over him and then began shaking him. He tried to push her away. This earned him a slap. She screamed, "Get up! We have to follow them!"

The blow instigated a thousand other aches, and he groaned as he raised an arm to feebly block another smack. She pummeled his defense, shrieking something he no longer fought to understand.

A shadow fell over them, and from behind his pitiful defense, he heard Mia grunting and demanding to be put down. Daring to peer through his guard, Thomas saw Hurstwell had carried her a few yards away. The gruff old soldier informed her, "That boy just about sacrificed his life to protect you. I know you want your sister back, but have some gratitude."

"We can't waste another moment. They're getting away!" Mia protested.

"Let's take a walk. Cool our heads before we act rashly."

No doubt another counter was on her lips, but Hurstwell had a way of moving one without them realizing they were being herded. Thomas glowered after Mia as Hurstwell led her off. With her gone, the aches had his full attention. He groaned and slumped back to the ground for several minutes before finally pulling himself together enough to stand.

Once up, Thomas noticed that Terrillian was still close by, examining some of their felled attackers. As Thomas stalked over stiffly, he counted ten of them.

Terrillian spoke up once Thomas reached his side. "There were enough to overtake me, about thirty total. But most of them suddenly left after I felled the first two. I heard Mia's sister scream but couldn't leave you and Mia."

"Thank you," Thomas choked out, unsure what else to say.

"They were like beasts in that there seemed no reasoning with them. But they were also less, because beasts have self-interest and more cunning."

A flicker of remembered terror as the vacant-eyed men pummeled him with their fists returned to Thomas. "Yeah," he said, his voice cracking.

Terrillian stood and put a hand on Thomas's shoulder. "You were very brave facing them with no weapon and outnumbered. Mia will see that in time."

Clearing his throat, Thomas asked, "What do you think made them attack? I saw a highwayman ambush some travelers once before. It was nothing like that."

Giving a shrug, Terrillian nodded in Hurstwell's direction. "Better to ask him. I've seen some pretty incredible and terrifying things, things I thought were legends. But truth is,

I'm new to the Order. I had only been considering pledging loyalty to the High King a few weeks before I had the vision."

"The vision?" Thomas asked, nudging one of their fallen attackers with his foot.

"Yeah. The High King comes to you to accept your pledge of fealty. Or maybe he comes and then you offer it. Maybe it's both. Like I said, I'm still really new to it all."

Thomas gestured to the bodies around them. "You seem like a pretty capable warrior to me. What did you do before?"

From deeper in the forest, he saw Mia walking back towards them with Hurstwell behind her as if blocking another potential flight. Terrillian waved to them and then muttered, "I worked in the mines at Ironhold."

"Iron-what? Where is—"

"We have to leave now," Mia interrupted. She was calling from a dozen yards away and had changed course slightly up the incline towards the road. "Those things don't look fast. We can surely overtake them."

"Milady," Hurstwell began.

"No, you convinced me to come back and not pursue her alone. But we aren't abandoning my sister. How could I face father knowing we let her be taken by who knows what villains!"

"I've served your father for twice your lifetime. Given the choice between losing one daughter or both, he would agree with me," Hurstwell replied though with greater control over his tone.

Mia was silent, looking like she was searching for anything to say back. Tears or fury looked equally possible alternatives.

"Do you know who these men might have been serving?" Terrillian spoke up.

"Isn't it obvious," she replied. "Maldes knows father is

supporting Viceroy Ecthelion. He sent those brutes to murder us!"

"Except they didn't murder your sister," Hurstwell said. "There's something amiss here."

"We have to get Delia back!" Mia insisted. She turned her eyes to Thomas. They shimmered with teary pleas.

He stiffened. Why did she expect him to side with her? After a few moments of her staring at him, he knew why. Rubbing his face, he conceded and spoke up, frustration edging his words. "Mia is right. Whatever the reason, we have to get Lady Delia and Gregor back."

At the mention of Gregor, Hurstwell grumbled. "You're all determined to be the death of me. Fine, master Thomas. Which way shall we go?"

"About a mile from here, there's a fork in the road. One way leads to Ecthalon and the other to Port Valence. If they're working for the Monarch, they'll be headed that way, no doubt."

"After the retreat, I doubt that road will be freely passable for us," Terrillian commented. "We could end up walking straight into irons ourselves."

Thomas could tell from the intensity in Mia's expression that wouldn't stop her, with or without them. "We could double back and cut across the battlefield. Head them off before they get to Ecthalon. So long as we press hard and are smart about it, we could flank them. I doubt they have anyone monitoring the forest after the way the battle turned out."

That last bit was a lie on Thomas's part, and he could tell from the way Hurstwell looked at him that he knew it. The old soldier just ran his tongue over his teeth and said, "Well, then we had best get moving, hadn't we?"

7

No one spoke throughout the trek into the forest apart from Thomas offering occasional whispered instructions. He was at the head of the column leading the way, though Hurstwell knew the way better than him. The old Knight had taken up the rearguard. It was pretty clear from the set of his stubbled jaw that he was trying to figure something out. Thomas had some guesses as to what. Chief among them the sudden cordiality between him and Mia. Ever since he had sided with her, she calmed. And followed close behind Thomas, rather than keeping as far as possible.

To an extent, Thomas wondered what had changed as well. He could understand Hurstwell's apprehensions. They excelled at their jobs when people behaved as expected.

"You know," Mia spoke up, her voice hushed and a little husky from their brisk trek. "You'll be a hero for this. She's going to swoon over you."

Thomas's cheeks reddened, and he took a bad step and bumped hard into a tree trunk. He quickly righted himself and grumbled, "I doubt that, she didn't even swoon over Mark. I'll be lucky to get a thank you."

He glanced back. Mia's lip twisted, not quite into a grimace but not a smile either. "Besides," he added, "This is your rescue. You think I'd work this hard to get Gregor back by my choosing?"

She tittered. "He does drive you crazy."

"Crazy isn't the half of it. I drive you crazy. He's on a whole other level."

When Thomas glanced back, he was surprised to see her scowling. "You don't drive me crazy."

She was surprisingly serious and insistent. Before Thomas could ask after it, a noise grabbed his attention.

"You can be annoying," she continued keeping her voice low as they had but still too loud.

"Mia," he whispered urgently as he peered through the thick trees and bushes and confirmed his suspicions. They were about to come onto the road on top of the kidnappers. At a checkpoint with soldiers of the Monarch, no less.

"But you do have your moments when—"

He turned and covered her mouth with his hand, making the sign for quiet. Fury and shock burned in her eyes. Mia probably wanted to bite his hand, but she complied.

Thomas stepped back and gestured placatingly to her before signaling to the others behind them to stop. Terrillian caught the message and relayed it to Hurstwell.

Turning his attention back to Mia, he mouthed, "They're just beyond the forest cover there."

Her eyes grew wide, and she started forward. He caught her by the arm just in time and shook his head. "No," he mouthed. "Soldiers. We need to hang back."

She responded with a furious shake that whipped her

humidity-frazzled hair around. "We're getting my sister and Gregor back."

Rubbing his face, Thomas motioned for her to stay put and crept back to the tree line to assess their options. He had a good vantage point, slightly higher than those he observed. The road was also very wide, offering him at least ten extra feet of distance from the nearest soldier. He could make out the words of one of the sentries. "You there, halt," he demanded of the slowly approaching convoy of the kidnappers. The group didn't break ranks or slow. At the center of party were two carriages, with Delia and Gregor presumably stowed in one. No doubt the other held the villain behind the whole sordid affair. On first blush, they looked like any other band of refugees or travelers. But Thomas recognized the same vacant expression on their faces as the fiends who had pummeled him earlier.

"This road has been secured by order of Maldes Ilyron, Monarch of Ecthelowall. Only loyalists may pass. Halt for an inspection."

The group still did not comply. They were almost on top of the quartet of soldiers. Their captain announced, "Halt, or we will be forced to restrain you by force. None may pass this point unchecked."

No discernible response to the threat was offered.

Nodding to his fellow soldiers, they drew swords and began to close ranks to intercept the kidnappers. Still no sign of slowing could be seen. They were steps apart.

"Now, see here," the lead soldier demanded. He pushed one of them backward and gave several steps as the kidnappers marched forward unfazed. Seeing this, the lead soldier shook his head and, with a swipe, dispatched the kidnapper directly in front of him. The man fell without seemingly breaking his stride, and his falling body knocked the lead soldier over.

Quicker than Thomas could process, the remaining group

of fifteen or so kidnappers changed from apathetic to destructive. All of them, with no concern for their lack of weapons or armor, fell upon the soldiers.

Those at the front were repulsed or cut down by the three standing soldiers, but others from the back and middle suddenly sprang to life with vicious fury and crashed like a human wave into the startled soldiers.

One of the soldiers cried out in terror.

Mia had come alongside Thomas. She let out a little gasp. "What are they doing?"

"They're like animals," Thomas observed, unsure how else to describe the frenzied attack. The soldiers cut down several more, but the abandon with which the strange kidnappers struck quickly turned the tide in their favor. Those who fell slumped like the first onto the soldier who slew them. This hobbled the defenders in their response for the next in line, which climbed over their compatriots. The creatures tore off the helmets of the soldiers before pounding their fists and clawing at them without mercy.

"What are they?" Thomas mumbled. "They're breaking their fists trying to batter and tear through the sentries' armor."

"Whoever they are, they have my sister, so I'm not just going to watch from here!"

"Wait a moment," Terrillian whispered as he joined them. "Look, a sentry managed to get his weapon drawn."

Sure enough, one of the pair had managed to throw off his attackers and stumbled to his feet. He swung his blade, cutting down one snarling, feral foe after another.

It was obvious there were too many for him. They were watching a last stand.

"This is a tragedy," Terrillian spoke up, not bothering to whisper.

"Agreed. I don't know what has bewitched those poor

fellows, but no nobles purse could compel such loyalty. Much less the pursuit of their honor."

"Their fate is tragic," Mia spoke up, giving each a stern look. "But my sister's fate is the one which most concerns me."

Thomas crept between the bushes he was looking through and half-skidded, half-walked down the hillside to the main road. He was sure the move surprised his fellow watchers on the ridge, but he knew this was where Mia's impulse would carry her if someone didn't act. Better he risk it than her. That he was chancing himself to keep Mia, who he'd detested, safe was something to unpack later.

The lone sentry was going down, this time for good, just as Thomas reached the road and dashed for the carriage. There were only five or so of the stiff walkers left standing. All of them were distracted with overwhelming the sentry. He made it inside the carriage and shut the door before any of them turned to see him.

As he entered the carriage, he had to duck. Over him, he glimpsed something metallic had glinted in the light from opening the carriage door. A moment later, he discovered the dagger's wielder was Delia. Her blue eyes glowered hard and vicious at him in the low light. "Woah, woah!" He managed to stammer out. "It's me, Thomas."

For a moment, Delia's gaze didn't soften. Out of the corner of his eye, Thomas noticed that Gregor lay sprawled across a bench of the carriage. Eyes closed, only the faintest of wheezing telling of life still in his limp body.

"Thomas, did you come alone?" Delia asked, her voice steady but with a note of uncertainty.

"No," Thomas replied, thinking a half-truth under the circumstance to be most expedient. "I have others with me. If you can walk, I think I can carry Gregor to safety before those creeps realize it."

Delia shook her head. "No, you're too late."

Before he could ask how she knew, the door behind him was thrust open, and he was dragged backward out of the carriage.

Two of her captors loomed over Thomas. They bore blank stares with only the faintest hint of displeasure curling their lips. Then they began ferociously kicking him.

Thomas curled into a ball immediately. But the injuries from his last beating, not even close to healed, reawakened with a fresh fury. His body jerked out of its protective shaping as he screeched in pain.

For just a second, he glimpsed Delia looking at him, a strange impassivity to her expression. She must have been resigned to his death and failure.

A kick found its way to his abdomen, and the wind was knocked from him in a gasp. This made the beating all the worse. He feared death, but dying like this, unable to breathe—but not drowning. Unable to fight back—but in the prime of his youth. This all seemed the cruelest jest the Lowlands had made of his life yet.

"Off him, you fiends!" Hurstwell bellowed and slung both attackers off with a hand on each. The two men wobbled and went down hard, landing on the ground and not moving. From the dirt, they stared back at him, mouths slack. Not dead, but were they truly alive? How very much like carrion they seemed to Thomas. Prey for something malevolent.

All his life, he had considered enchantments and spells to be malarkey. Something for the superstitious to make otherwise callous and banal existences more interesting. Looking into those deadened eyes, he wondered if he had been wrong.

The piteous creatures moaned and hauled themselves to their feet, ignoring what should have been the pain of contusions and lacerations. They also paid no heed to

Hurstwell's bared blade, which Thomas thought also had a faint shimmering as of heat around it.

"I give you each one warning. Depart, or I shan't spare either of you," Hurstwell cautioned.

Both carrion-men advanced. A minute later, they dropped, one after the other, as Hurstwell kept his word.

Thomas stared at them from where he lay. In death, they looked much like they had moments before in life, which decided it for him. Carrion was the term he would use for these strange men they had encountered. He'd be sure to exaggerate and exonerate none of their horror when relating the tale of this in the future. Presuming he managed to escape the Monarch's forces and his injuries long enough to do so.

"That was a foolish thing to do," Hurstwell chided as he hauled Thomas to his feet. He threw in a grunt as if affirmed when Thomas winced and groaned.

"I was going for brave and daring," he countered.

He glanced at Delia, hoping to find some support from her, but her expression was hard to read. She looked lost in thought with a furrow on her brow.

She must have realized he was staring at her because she suddenly blinked and then gave a reproving smile. "It was both, I'd say." Then her gaze traveled up, and she exclaimed, "Sister!"

Mia didn't break stride as she dashed the final steps up into the carriage and hugged Delia.

Mia had tears on her cheeks as she spoke fast as a hummingbird's wings, "I thought I had lost you to those brutes! And with Father gone ... well, maybe gone. He might be in Port Valence with the Viceroy. But he could be dead, like Mother, and I couldn't bear—"

"He's in Port Valence with the Viceroy?" Delia interrupted, sounding intrigued more than enthusiastic.

"We don't know for sure. The battlefield was awful. That thug Thomas had to all but carry me away."

"Thug?" Thomas protested though no one seemed to notice.

"No, not Father, the Viceroy," Delia clarified sharply.

"Oh, well, yes. But Father—"

"Is in Port Valence, I knew that."

"But, how? We both were told he'd be at the battlefield?"

"Oh," Delia replied quickly, a momentary flush on her face. "Those, um, highwaymen, mentioned it as part of their scheme to ransom me."

"Oh, Deli, that's awful," Mia mewled.

Delia squeezed her sister. "We have so much to be thankful for! You have rescued me, and now we know both Father and the Viceroy are safe as well. We should head to Port Valence at once."

"Remember, we shouldn't go straightway to Port Valence," Terrillian spoke up.

Thomas whirled to see the other teen, caught off guard by his presence. To his back, Delia responded coolly, "Who is this?"

"Oh, yes. This is Sir Terrillian, a Knight of Light from Libertias," Mia answered. "We found him on the battlefield at Primrose Glade while looking for signs of Father."

"A pleasure to make your acquaintance, Lady Delia." Terrillian offered his hand to her.

Delia sneered at the offering. Thomas guessed because it was both informal and Libertian in nature. "How do we know we can trust this knight who happened to be the only survivor of the battle? What if he's a servant of the Monarch, sent to dupe us? This isn't an hour for questionable alliances."

Mia gaped at first and flushed. Then her brows furrowed as she regarded Terrillian. To Thomas, she seemed to be vacillating between outright denial and seriously considering the charge.

"He helped get us to you safely, Lady Delia. We would not have succeeded had he not," Thomas pointed out. "If betrayal was his aim, he had opportunity enough."

There was a fractional narrowing of Delia's eyes before she let a smile rest on her lips. "I suppose I shouldn't be surprised such wise counsel came from you, Thomas. You're right, of course. It would be rather astonishing for him to have orchestrated such a complex ruse."

"It would have to be a meandering and misguided ruse," Mia said with a laugh. One which Delia shortly reciprocated airily.

"Indeed," Terrillian added in, seemingly unabashed by the joke effectively at his expense. "So, is there any objection to taking the route I propose? That way we can ferret out any pursuers before we rejoin the Viceroy?"

"Pursuers are precisely why we must make all haste to reach Port Valence at once!" Delia countered. "Who knows what may befall us. Think of poor Gregor! He needs medical attention and is the only remaining heir to the throne."

"He's not the only heir," Thomas grumbled mostly to himself. A heavy hand on his shoulder quieted him.

"Then let's get to the road with all haste," Hurstwell proposed. "I'd rather not skulk in these woods longer than I need. Too many strange happenings here for my liking." To Terrillian, he added, "Will you accompany us, Sir Terrillian?"

Sighing, he shrugged. "I will go where needed."

"Well said," Hurstwell replied. With that, the group began to clear the fallen carrion and get the horses turned about to make for the port. Mia climbed into the carriage with Delia and Gregor and shut the door.

Some minutes into the trek, Hurstwell walked alongside

Thomas and whispered, "Something is off. How did Delia know no one survived the battle? I didn't even know that, and I've been with you since your visit there."

"I don't know. What does it matter?" Thomas whispered back.

"Oh, perhaps naught at all. Just musing," Hurstwell said and walked on.

It wasn't like Hurstwell to keep his confidence that way. Not with Thomas, at least. They spoke freely or not at all to one another. It was what made serving under the soldier worthwhile. If he was into the market for secrets now, then that was just one more perplexing weight added to this bizarre day.

8

———

Thomas wiped fresh beads of sweat from his brow. Shielding his eyes, he peered ahead some hundred or more yards to Port Valence's gates. Scores of people lined along the road were barring access to the only entry point left to the city.

"How did they get word to so many of the Viceroy's supporters?" he muttered to Hurstwell, who wiped his face with his cape.

"News of a defeat like Cromwell Forest travels fast. It's possible they sent out riders to warn everyone."

"Is an evacuation of the area really needed?" Terrillian strode up from his turn sitting as driver for the carriage that hadn't moved in close to an hour.

"There are rumors from the early battles farther north along the Milis River that the Monarch does not treat citizens who support the Restoration kindly," Hurstwell grumbled, his voice low. "Rumors travel faster than truth."

"That still doesn't explain why they're taking so long to let everyone in," Thomas peered behind them. The line stretched into the distance for hundreds more yards and then over a hill and beyond what he could see.

"They're no doubt testing everyone who comes to the gate, confiscating weapons, and the like. With this big an influx of people, there's no telling who they could be letting in. Too many Monarchists stowed in the bunch of us, and they could take the gate and open it during an impending attack. Sink ships. Assassinate our nobles ..." Hurstwell trailed off as he looked meaningfully at the carriage.

Delia and Mia must be roasting in there but had to stay inside for safety. They still didn't know who the kidnappers worked for, and Gregor still hadn't woken, which was worrisome. A scowl formed on Thomas's face. "Maybe I should double back and fill our skins with water? Make sure none of us get dehydrated."

Stroking his beard and then wiping away sweat once more, Hurstwell said, "Hm, very well. We passed a calm stream that forked off the Greenstrand River about a mile back. You could fill them there and return before we've moved a foot, I daresay."

With a nod, Thomas ran to the carriage and rapped on the door. It swung open, and from the rush of heat, he knew he was right about the sweltering conditions within. Even so, when Delia leaned out, the sweat did not seem to soak her hair or streak her face but give it a glistening quality like a warm dew. It took him a moment to find his words.

"Um, Lady Delia, I apologize for troubling you, but if you would permit me, I'd like to take your and Mia's waterskins to be refilled."

A small smile quirked up the corner of Delia's mouth. "Ever the gentleman, Thomas. Just like Mark. Yes, please do refill them. Though on one condition."

Thomas's brows knit. "Yes?"

"You must finish the rest of what's in my skin before you

leave. Running and fighting for my sister and my safety all day must surely have taken its toll. Please, drink this for me and ease my mind?"

He almost protested, but propriety and practicality both died on his lips at the sight of the pleading in her eyes. "Of course, Lady Delia. Thank you for such a thoughtful gesture." For just a moment his eyes shot past her to see Mia. Arms folded over her chest; a glower set firmly on her face.

Mia's eyes caught his, and she looked away. "Delia, you can have the rest of mine. If you can be generous, so can I."

Taking Delia's waterskin and draining it—it still had about a quarter of its contents—Thomas waited for Delia and Mia to sort out the other skin. After a minute of negotiating, it was settled Thomas would have hers too. He thanked both sisters and quickly hurried back to Hurstwell, admittedly much better hydrated than before and with spirits far higher.

Hurstwell grunted as he approached. "Wipe the grin off your face. It will draw notice if you're smug while all around us are so dour. Better yet, keep a dose of what caused that dourness in your thoughts."

Biting his lip, Thomas nodded, "Yes, sir."

Another load of water skins was handed to Thomas. "Take Sir Terrillian with you. In case anyone takes issue with you passing them up to return to us."

"Right," Thomas replied though he suspected the old soldier was up to something. Perhaps he still didn't trust Terrillian. After all, they'd known him for only half of one of the craziest days of any of their lives. The message unspoken seemed clear: "Keep an eye on him."

Thomas motioned to Terrillian to follow. "There's a brook off the main river nearby we can use to fill these."

At first, Terrillian didn't respond. He stared into the distance, seemingly dumbfounded by Port Valence. Thomas understood why. Ahead, the verdant grassy meadow stretched from the wood line to the city's white walls. All along the coast the magnificent weathered stone faces plunged sheer into the frothy sea beneath. But the city was cradled in the only lull in the Wellingsly Cliffs. The buildings stood like thin, pointed towers and filled every bit of the space accorded. Beyond was rolling waves as far as one looked. It gave the impression the land wore a crown of stone atop azul streaming locks. This was only enhanced by the enormous falls the Greenstrand created a half mile down the coast. Near enough, in fact, for Thomas to hear the faint echoes of their perpetual, defiant roar.

"If you like how it looks now, wait till twilight arrives. I'm told it's truly breathtaking then," Thomas commented.

Terrillian smirked. "Looks like I'll get to see it from this spot too."

Despite the depth of his distraction, he walked over to Thomas and kept going toward the brook. Thomas matched step, and they continued in silence until they reached the tree line.

"So, you're quite smitten with Lady Delia, it seems," Terrillian commented as though trying to suss out a riddle.

Thomas felt his cheeks warm. "No! Well, I suppose so. I mean, who in the Lowlands wouldn't be?"

The Libertian teen shrugged. "I know one."

"Who, you?" Thomas pressed.

They walked a bit further before he cocked his head towards Thomas and said, "Besides, I think you and Mia are good for each other."

"Mia?" On impulse, Thomas almost added, "The troll?" Fortunately, he caught himself. He started the day freely able to say such a thing, but their time in the woods complicated that sentiment. It set him out of sorts, like hearing a strange sound in the depths of the night. "There's no use in thinking of either of them. Delia is betrothed to Gregor, and Mia will be matched to a lesser noble. Meanwhile, I'll be opening doors for them and standing watch while their husbands go hunting or some other ridiculous nonsense."

"Do they not have any say in it?" Terrillian asked, sounding genuinely surprised.

"Not really. Perhaps Delia chose her first fiancé, Mark. He was someone special. I think she genuinely cared about him. But in general, matches are made based on mutual benefit to the houses of the couple."

"That's a shame," was all Terrillian responded.

Thomas stopped. His companion cut off the path into some trees before the clearing where they could access the brook readily. Besides being suspicious, that ill ease he felt quickly fomented into annoyance. "What, do you think love drives anything in the Lowlands? If I remember rightly, the only tie that bound my parents was a cool understanding. But had they not died, both their houses would have reaped a benefit in me."

The words tasted awful in his mouth. They were true. They were impossible now. But most of all, when he saw the pitying expression on Terrillian's face, they felt hollow. Inadequate. The fullest description of himself.

"You asked if I knew anyone in the Lowlands who could resist Delia's charms. One of my friends and fellow Knight, Anargen, is who I was thinking about. When we set out on our quest for the High King, he left behind the girl he loved, Seren. In the midst of everything we faced, he never stopped thinking of her. He wrote several letters. I think if Delia were to offer him all the riches of the Lowlands with herself, he wouldn't sway an inch from choosing Seren. Love isn't expedient for profit in gold, but it overcomes the insurmountable."

There was silence between them and neither moved. It lingered so long that Thomas began to chaff under his inability to find something in response because he felt certain one had been prompted by Terrillian's bold declaration.

At length, Terrillian ducked under a tree limb and started cutting a path down the gentle slope off the road heading towards the stony depression of the brook. Thomas followed mutely. They had walked maybe a mile and a half further when Terrillian spoke up. "This has been quite a day."

Thomas looked at him quizzically because the other teen had delivered his lofty philosophizing so deadpan that he wasn't sure whether to take it as a joke or seriously. When no added sign of intent given, he replied, "It has, though I suppose fighting for the Viceroy and the Restoration you've seen worse."

From the way Terrillian's eyebrows lifted, he hadn't expected that response either. "Actually, no. There's only ever been one time that I've felt so completely out of control. And that definitely wasn't while here in ..."

The teen trailed off as they reached the stream. Its steady, gentle voice as it flowed over the smooth stones were hardly what interrupted his thoughts. "It was before coming here?" Thomas surmised.

"Yeah," Terrillian replied, again in that strange pensiveness. "Ordumair."

"The Siege? You mentioned it before. Was it especially brutal?"

There was no answer. It was as though Terrillian hadn't heard him, perhaps couldn't even see Thomas for how he stared off into the distance. Brow furrowed, Thomas made his way across the bigger stones to a place where he could bend down and began collecting the water. It wasn't as easy here as the spot he had in mind, but it would do. All the while, he kept a wary eye on his strangely erratic companion.

All of a sudden, Terrillian seemed to snap back. "We have

to get back," he said and began edging along the bank of the stream in the opposite direction of Port Valence.

"Uh okay, but it's actually the other way. We came from—"

"Shh," he shushed, a gentle request rather than a brusque demand. Thomas fell silent, more out of confusion than compliance. What was he doing?

Thomas followed for a bit and was about to ask after Terrillian's sanity when he heard a yelp of pain from beyond the trees and shrubs back where the main road wound through the wood to the open seacoast. Terrillian peered through some branches and motioned him over.

Through the thick gnarls of willow saplings laden with honeysuckle, Thomas saw two of the sentries along the road for the Restoration. Their group had passed this checkpoint on the way to Port Valence. Now they were both on the ground with Monarchist soldiers standing over them, fresh blood dripping down the blade.

"You're sure they won't send a change of sentries before nightfall?" One of the two enemy soldiers inquired.

"We both know how sentry duty works. They change them four times a day. This pair had just gone on duty. We're in the clear to move everyone into position for the assault."

"Then that's it. The war is about to end."

"Only if Admiral Gelccer brings his fleet in to block a retreat. If the Viceroy escapes, who knows who might harbor him and support the cause. Libertias and Rehalcy certainly won't shed tears if Ecthelowall tears itself apart."

"Mm, and they pick up the pieces," the other agreed. "Do you want to report back or me?"

"Better you go. I'm a sharper lookout."

The other man gave him a shove, "You mean you're lazier. Fine. Don't go to sleep, you lout. I have a feeling everything is going to go as planned, and this time tomorrow we'll be celebrating the Restoration's surrender!"

A minute or more elapsed and Thomas couldn't bring himself to move. He hardly dared to breathe. The exchange had been so casual but spelled doom for him and everyone he'd ever known. None of the nobles who sided with the Viceroy were likely to be allowed to live. They would be traitors to the crown. He had heard about such purges in Knorland's duchies when a First Duke would seize power. The dukes of each Knor duchy were executed, along with their families, to make room for loyalist replacements. He and Hurstwell might skirt such a cleansing, particularly if they fled now. But Delia, Mia, and even that pain Gregor would surely die. How would he live with it if he abandoned them to that fate and escaped?

Beside Thomas, a sudden motion startled him. Had the monarchist spotted them?

No, Terrillian was bursting through the brush. Before Thomas could warn against it, the Knight had overtaken the monarchist and rendered him unconscious.

Gaping, Thomas wandered across the road to stand beside the other teen. He wanted to say something, but all he could do was wonder fruitlessly after how Terrillian had known to hide and strike when he had. More than that how he continued to effortlessly defeat foes. It was as if the heroic warrior Cinaed of Tislatna had returned to life and stood before him. He stared fixedly at the silvery armor aglow with the flaming ancient words.

"We need to get back to the others and warn them," Terrillian asserted as he pulled the body off the path. "The refugees will need to be brought into the city at once."

"Of course," Thomas said, giving his head a slight shake. It didn't help make any of this more real nor lessen the imminence of the danger they faced.

Faster than he was prepared for, Terrillian was off, dashing back down the road towards Port Valence. Thomas drew in a breath and prepared to try to catch him when he heard a crack of a rifle. He turned to see the other Monarchist headed toward him. He must have had a further word for the other soldier. Panic seized Thomas and gave his legs all the speed he had doubted he had.

9

Weaving through the dozens still in line to enter the city, Thomas barely noticed the curses and slurs leveled at him for "skipping the line." Terrillian was several yards ahead in their sprint back to the others. By the time he reached them, Terrillian was already explaining the situation.

"If we don't get these people into the city and the gate shut, they'll be massacred," Terrillian finished.

Hurstwell stroked his chin in thought as Thomas tried to approach as quietly as possible. All the same, Mia noticed him from the carriage and smirked. She mouthed, "Slow foot."

Thomas scowled back at her. What was with her? Had she forgotten everything between them at the glade?

"Thomas!" Hurstwell chided.

"Yes, sir," he replied, startled.

The gruff Knight's brows knitted. "Pay attention. You understood everything to be just as Terrillian had?"

"Yes, sir," he answered though he couldn't help glancing at Terrillian uncertainly for a second. He wanted to tell them about the other soldier coming back, but he was still struggling to get the breath to form the warning.

"Very well," Hurstwell said with a sigh, cutting off Thomas's chance to speak. "My lady," he addressed Delia. "We must get you into the city at once. Please come with me."

Delia reached out her hand and was helped down. Hurstwell came around to the horses and uncoupled them from the carriage. He led one around and helped Delia onto it. Then he climbed into the carriage and remerged with Gregor's limp form in his arms.

Somehow, he managed to mount the other horse with the boy in his arms. He instructed Thomas, "You must bring Miss Mia as quickly as possible. I will get Lady Delia to the keep and alert the guard. Don't dawdle."

With that, he nodded to Delia and spurred his horse on. The pair raced away, surprising a few standers-by as they did.

The whole exchange happened so fast; Thomas didn't have a chance to ask how he would coax the gatekeepers into letting them in. Perhaps his unexpressed warning of being spotted would be enough.

"I can't believe he left me with you," Mia commented almost absently. Though for her expression she may as well have been standing amid a pile or manure as the tall swaying beach grasses.

Heat rose in Thomas's cheeks and found a path to his tongue, "It's not like I—"

"He couldn't spare room on the horses," Terrillian interrupted, shooting Thomas a pointed look.

Was that what Mia had meant? Thomas swallowed uncomfortably and looked back. His eyes widened in horror. They were a long way off yet, but he could see people running and hear the growing collective cry of panic. The Monarch's forces had arrived.

10

Thomas grabbed Mia's hand without thinking and dashed off toward the gate of the city. He dimly registered her initial complaints, but they must have died off when the panic in the refugee crowd became apparent. It was impossible to know for sure, all he could hear was the din of frantic shouts. They had a head start on hundreds, but there were many ahead of them already turning to see the commotion and fleeing themselves.

Tall grasses whipped his limbs as he fought to move faster and faster. It would never be fast enough, he already knew. He could see the guards had spotted the commotion. They were shouldering people down. One threatened to use his halberd. Behind him, someone tried to shut the gates to the city.

"No, no, no," Thomas gasped out as they closed the last thirty yards.

The gates were forced to stay open as the terrified villagers pushed over the soldiers and streamed into the city. A minute later, Thomas passed under the gatehouse and into the frantic streets of Port Valence. Those who had been waiting outside the walls dashed to and fro in a panic as the citizens of the port city cried out in surprise and added to the chaos. Down the street, an older man was knocked through the glass pane of a shop's window. The rare luxury shattered horrifically and he jerked Mia after him, determined not to see what became of the man or those around it.

He made his way through the winding streets, taking lefts and rights with no sense of direction. The goal was to get away. Sir Hurstwell had to be close. He hadn't been gone that long. Where had he gone? Had he left directions to follow? It all happened so fast.

His head swam. There had to be someplace quiet and safe enough to catch his breath and think clearly. Just for a moment. That's all Thomas needed.

Dimly he registered Mia's voice rising to a yell.

Finally, he whirled to a stop when she shouted, "You're tearing my wrist apart!" and jerked her hand free.

His first instinct was to grab it again, worried they would be separated by the throngs. Instead of finding the panicked masses around him, he realized they were on a street deeper in the city, and the citizens here were mostly looking at him as the source of concern.

Thomas nodded and tried to steady his breathing. "I'm sorry," he wheezed.

Mia gingerly nursed her reddened wrist. "Me too." Her expression softened after a moment, perhaps because he looked in no shape to fight back right now. "Do you have any idea where you're taking us?" she asked. Gently, she shoved him towards a side alley away out of the open. Sounds of the commotion at the gate were beginning to reach here. Wherever that was.

Thomas rubbed his face. "No," he admitted. "I've only been here once before, when I was small."

"Why the blazes did you drag me like a doll through the streets then?" Mia snapped.

"I ... had to get you to safety. Get us to safety," he amended.

Blinking her eyes, an inscrutable riddle in her green-eyed gaze, she eventually sighed. "I think I can get us to the keep. Can you pull yourself together enough to at least pretend to be the escort to a Lady of Ecthelowall?"

Fear and fatigue had buried the fight in him deep enough that he took the barb without resistance. "Having Terrillian will help with—wait, where is he?"

Amid the tall stalwart, white edifices all around, Terrillian was notably absent. When had they lost him? In the field getting into the city? In the throngs trampling each other? Where was he?

"With everyone bashing into one another and clamoring to get away over each other, it's a wonder we were able to make it here together."

Involuntarily he glanced down at her wrist. His cheeks reddened, and he quickly mumbled. "We'll have to double back and help him."

A group of Restoration soldiers pushed past them. Thomas gaped as they barely slowed their pace up the inclined street. How had he missed the change in elevation?

Mia grabbed his hand and gave it a yank. "Come on, let's follow them!"

Without giving him time to seriously agree or disagree, they were off. To her credit, the idea worked to get them back to the city's main gate. Upon reaching it, Thomas wished it hadn't.

Monarchist soldiers were already pressing to get in. Bodies from villagers, defenders, and attackers lay strewn about. Sounds of arrows twanging and rifle shots from atop the wall competed with the song of steel-on-steel and soldiers' shouts.

This was the last place he should've brought Mia. From on

the wall, someone cried out and came crashing to the street nearby. One of the invaders had scaled a siege ladder and tossed down the wall sentry he'd encountered. More of his kind began mounting the wall and spreading.

"They're going to take the city," he muttered.

"What?" Mia shouted in the din, her eyes flashing with fear and uncertainty.

"I have to get you out of here!" He grabbed her arm to pull her again and felt her struggle against his hold.

"Look, over there," she insisted, "I see him!"

Thomas traced the direction Mia emphatically pointed. Sure enough, there Terrillian stood valiantly battering aside foes on each side.

He held flaming spiritswords in each hand; a small buckler adorned one arm and crackled alike. On the little shield was the face of a lion. Or perhaps a lamb with a star behind it. Whatever the case, a crossbow bolt plinked off it as though hitting a castle wall and, with a whirl, he dispatched the crossbowman and another two infantrymen before they could get five feet past the gatehouse.

"Watch out!" Mia jerked Thomas back.

He flailed his arms and went down hard. Wincing he saw stone crumbling from where a rifle ball had just struck the wall of the building they had been in front of. "Thanks," he murmured, trying to pull himself together. Little good it did. He felt like he was trapped under the surface of an iced-over pond.

"Where are you right now?" Mia snapped. "I need you here, not daydreaming about Delia."

Though he knew he should be angry about the insinuation, he couldn't muster it. The icy glaze over his thoughts was too thick.

"I ..." Nothing more would come.

She shook him. "Thomas, stop playing games. Get up!"

Something was very wrong. His limbs were heavy. As though the more he mentally fought to stir, to move, to do anything, the further he sank.

"Thomas? Thomas?" Mia cried, possibly still shaking him. Her voice sounded farther and farther away.

Then all of the voices and sounds grew faint and Thomas realized his eyes must have shut, because he couldn't see. He couldn't feel Mia shaking him nor the sweat rolling down his brows nor the thrum of his own frantic heartbeat. Only his internal thoughts were left to him, and they were increasingly disjointed and slippery. Like trying to grab a fish underwater. The last he could wrangle made no sense.

All is. Dark. In this. Day...

Pain erupted like a long-dormant volcano sending tremors through his body. With a scream, he tried to grab his chest, but his arms were numb and limp at his sides. It burned so badly! Worse, the burning was spreading from his chest outward. Arms, legs, head, all of it ached with the fiery sensation.

His eyes cleared or opened or both. He couldn't tell which. Before him stood Terrillian in his brilliant burning armor. One sword pointed right at Thomas's chest. No, held to his chest!

Flames were leaping off it and tracing along Thomas's body, sinking fiery pinions into his flesh. Thomas yelped in pain. He reached out to push away the sword, but for some reason could not bring himself to remove its touch. The burning was so painful in his limbs and head, but his torso no longer hurt.

He stared up at Terrillian, who offered a wan smile.

The fire seemed to be awakening all his being to the world again. In the next moment, the sounds and chaos of the scene around them hit him.

They were no longer near the gate but instead somewhere

deeper in the city. Though his throat felt raw and dry, he asked, "Where are we?"

"A few streets away from the gatehouse," Terrillian answered.

"Sir Terrillian carried you here. I thought for sure you had been shot and were dying on me," Mia said, her voice and gestures almost too quick to follow. "And then he laid his sword on you and it looked like it was setting you on fire—"

Terrillian put a hand on her shoulder and said, "He'll be fine. The Spiritsword has burned away the dark sorceries strangling him."

"Sorceries?" Thomas and Mia asked almost in unison.

Terrillian glanced around, then nodded. "There was a dark pall over your skin. I noticed deep shadows around your face earlier, but thought it might have been a trick of the light through the trees. When Mia brought me to you, I could feel the righteous indignation of the Great King against the shadows strangling you. I don't know who or when it happened, but I think you were poisoned."

Struggling to sit up, Thomas gaped. "Poisoned? Dark magics?" He felt his bracing arm threaten to buckle. Mia was there in an instant to help shore him up.

"Whatever it was, I'm just glad I don't have to drag you to the keep," Mia said. The strain in her voice made the joke come off as forced. It also felt strange to have her so close. After his loss of sensation, the warmth of her body and the vigorous thrum of her heart were strangely comforting.

Thomas's eyes roved to the Spiritsword in Terrillian's hand, with its razor-sharp point that had conducted the fiery cure into him moments ago. Its gleaming surface still glowed fervently with the flames Thomas thought only a myth until today. Something about the sword beckoned to him. He had the strangest inclination to reach out and touch its burning surfaces. Half-consciously, he raised his hand to do just that as the faintest echo of some spoken words too muted and foreign to be fully comprehended gained volume in his ear.

"Let's get you to your feet," Mia announced. "Who knows how long they'll be able to hold the gate."

Blinking, Thomas nodded, "Right. We have to get to the keep." Feeling his strength already much returned, it didn't take much assistance from Mia.

For his part, Terrillian didn't offer to help or speak until Thomas was on his feet again. He smacked his lips which had been pursed in a thoughtful expression. "You're right. I have to get back to the gate and help hold the line." He turned to leave but hesitated, likely having seen the protest building in Thomas's expression before he could form the words for them.

"I was sent here to fight for the safety of the real Ecthelowall," Terrillian said. "Don't worry about me.

"You, on the other hand," he addressed Thomas, "Need this," he held out one of his two spiritswords, hilt first.

Eyes wide with surprise and a bit of wonder, Thomas shook his head. "I couldn't. If you're going to defend the gate, you'll need all your arms and prowess."

Terrillian chuckled. "I'm sure I will, but I've never been great at fighting with two blades. To be honest, I've been wondering why my mentor Sir Cinaed gave it to me in the first place. Strange as it sounds, I think it's meant for you."

With an eagerness balanced by trepidation and the weight of years of suspicion for such things, Thomas took the sword. "Thank you," he intoned solemnly, feeling like he was in some sort of ritual or ceremony.

"May the High King's favor be upon you, and his fire guard your steps," Terrillian said and then slid the faceplate of his helmet in place and took off up the street and back in what Thomas realized was the direction from which all manner of chaotic sounds issued. The world was coming more and more into focus for him, particularly the weight and peculiar warmth of the sword he now gripped.

Mia tugged at his arm. "Strange and a stranger as he might have been, I wonder if we should stop him."

Thomas shook his head. "No, he has his task before him. And I have mine. It's my duty to deliver you to safety."

"Ha," Mia chortled. "I think I'm the one who has been 'delivering' you."

He rolled his eyes, in part because there was a strange earnestness to Mia's proclamation. Feeling a foreign heaviness hanging between them, Thomas decided to let it go. "Fine, but if anyone asks, I'm going to say I led you straightway to the keep."

Raising her eyebrows, Mia stared at him. Expectant.

He sighed. "Lead the way." Oddly, her grin sent a twinge of satisfaction through him.

11

Standing in the servants' corridor within Port Valence's keep, Thomas understood why he hadn't been able to get a bearing on the structure's location. Beyond his mystical poisoning—the nature of which he was still skeptical about—there was no spotting it from where he'd been. The keep wasn't at the highest point like many other fortified cities. Instead, the soaring cliffs and solidarity of Ecthelowall's ancient claims to the lands around Port Valence had led its defensive architects to focus on repelling invaders from the sea. As such, its castle and keep were built wrapped in the arms of its harbor. The sea breaking against its stalwart grey stones, dozens of feet below the castle, made one of the most unique, impressive fortifications Thomas had ever seen. And the most disheartening. Môrmawr Castle, as it was named, boasted two towers loaded with ballista, two more with modern mortars, and cannons lining its curtain wall. All of which deterred invaders from the sea. But the slopes worked against Môrmawr when attacked from land. If the defenses at the city's gate fell, the invaders would have the high ground and almost certainly overthrow the castle in less than a day.

Knowing the tenuous position they were in made being stuck here, "where he belonged," all the more painful. Hurstwell had given him an apologetic look when he'd been ushered out of the main hall after delivering Mia. He had earned a place at the tables where the strategy for winning the day was discussed. When he presented Mia to the group, Delia had rushed over, kissed him on the cheek, and declared him a hero. It was at that moment Mia decided to unceremoniously skewer him by revealing she had rescued him more so than the other way around.

Thomas bet that would spawn some boisterous jokes at his expense from those in the room later. And if not among them, then certainly among the other watchmen and guards with whom he'd have to share shifts at watch.

Pity no one kept court like in the old days. He was shaping up to be a prime apprentice for the court jester. "With my luck as it's been, Gregor will become Monarch, and that's exactly what I'll be. His court jester."

A pang of guilt hit him. It wasn't right to speak that way, particularly not this moment. Not when Gregor was as still as the grave, and the Mayor of Valence's physicians had already exhausted their craft to no avail.

Had his father not bankrupted his family by investing so heavily in the merchant fleet that was destroyed in reprisals for Ecthelowall's privateering, Thomas might be the one engaged to Delia. Part of him ached with longing at that notion. Another part he couldn't ignore found that unthinkable. He chalked that up to feeling like he had betrayed Mark's memory with the thought.

Sighing, he produced the spiritsword Terrillian had given

him. It was a long sword and a little broader than any swords he had practiced with. Because of the war, he wasn't even accorded a dagger for his duties. Then again, he was never assigned any task for which Hurstwell wasn't present. Hurstwell could be aptly called Armed-well. It was good to be entrusted with something valuable like this. Even if, in his hands, its silvery surfaces didn't quite gleam the way they did in Terrillian's hands. Nor did the inscriptions glow white hot and issue flames that enwrapped the blade. He traced some of the words inscribed on it, repeating them softly to himself as he did. Midway through "I fear no danger, for the Hight King is with me," he felt something sting his finger and he yelped. His eyes widened. There were ruddy hues shimmering within the lettering on the spiritsword that gave off heat.

He wanted to drop it. He couldn't bear to drop it. Then everything went black.

Black, but not dark, because he could see clearly. At first, he was alone in a wide clearing, reminiscent of Primrose Glade. In the distance was an indistinct shape against the horizon. It was bitter cold, though without wind or any sign of winter. "Where am I?"

A sound like thunder boomed, resounding as though he were in a cave instead of a tableland. To Thomas's wonder, he understood the thunder as words. He found his legs obeying almost on their own, and he walked until he saw the shape of a tower. It had at its top a light that burned low. All around, the fading embers of the tower's light high above cast a preternatural auburn pall upon the area all around its base. It set his nerves on edge, but even at the periphery of the light's touch, he knew it accorded precious warmth. But the thunder spoke again, and he knew he could not enter the light's enclosure.

As the light faded, its circle of radiance retracted. It was then Thomas noticed something stirring. Looking through the light cast by the tower, he could see ... things. Monstrous things, hideous and numerous, such as he had never dared encounter in his most horrific nightmares. These creatures were edging towards the tower as its luminous dominion diminished. Thomas shifted his position and realized that it was only through the tower's light that he could see the encroaching army. The hairs on his neck stood on end. Though he could not see them, he was also surrounded by a fiendish horde.

Thomas began swaying. The terror had slipped inch by icy inch into his bones, and he thought for sure he would drop dead from fright. But the thunder boomed and pulled his attention back to the tower. Somehow its light had faltered so much since he last looked that no aura of protective light now existed. Instead, four figures of light stood on each side in defense of the tower.

All at once a feral cry, wicked and wild, went up from all around, and all the terrible creatures once hidden were revealed. They converged on the tower and its sentinels. Some beasts clambered up the sides of the protectors; others smashed into them and the tower, over and over. Sounds of stone cracking began to mix with gleeful revelry expressed by the creatures in growls and hisses and voices disgustingly sweet and disastrously acerbic. Desperation seized Thomas's heart. Somehow, he knew if the tower fell, all would be lost. And Thomas stood watching the end of all good, completely incapable of staying the ruinous tide.

The thunder boomed louder than before. Pulling not only his eyes but the eyes of all those against the tower to it. Above the tower, a vortical storm of lightning-streaked clouds glowered on the assembled enemies below, and with a sound like a rushing waterfall or dam breaking forth, the storm alit with fire and burst forth onto tower, setting the tower's beacon ablaze with a flash of light and heat so powerful it blew Thomas off of his feet. Thomas closed his eyes, certain the splendor alone would kill him.

Instead, the heat faded with a suddenness that left him frigid. He dared not open his eyes again until the salty scent of the sea and the tepid balminess of Port Valence edged into his senses and bid him to chance it. Looking around, all was the same as before, except the perspective was off. It took a moment to realize the one thing different about the room was that he was lying on the rough stone floor, curled up tight.

What had he just seen? Was it an after-effect of his poisoning?

A thought that did not feel as though it had originated with him pressed fiercely into his consciousness. The one part of him not curled in fear was an outstretched arm. In its hand clenched the spiritsword. Warmth radiated from it, and he had the distinct impression it had told him what he'd just experienced was a vision.

The term vision tangled in conjured imaginings of the Oracles of Tislatna and other mythical fancies along with charlatan soothsayers. But no, this was different. How he knew it to be different was as mysterious as the vision itself.

A sudden sound shattered the stillness of his inward thoughts. It was followed by another and another like it. A faint tremor ran through the stones of the hall. Canon fire.

Thomas stumbled to his feet and sheathed the spiritsword. What had prompted the castle's canons to fire, and how had he felt it here when the shots came from the towers? It would be risky trying to bombard the Monarchist positions in the city from here.

A moment later, Hurstwell burst into the hall. "Thomas!"

"Yes, sir," he replied and rushed over. The older man's face was lined with worry, and his jaw was tensed like he'd received a grievous wound.

"Come with me. We have to get Gregor to the boats right away."

Hurstwell headed down the hall to the room where Gregor was being tended to.

"Are we taking him to Castle Yerst by ship?"

Hurstwell didn't slow until they reached the room's door. "No. The castle is under siege. We're evacuating him and as much of the Restoration to New Ecthelowall."

Gaping, Thomas shook his head slowly. "It's too soon! How did the Monarchists break through so quickly? It should've taken a day or more at least."

Hurstwell sighed. "It should have, and we don't have any details as yet. We just know the lines broke and now they're bombarding the castle from the city. You and Terrillian said they were waiting for Admiral Gelccer to pin us in. If we sail now, we should make it to Merlais before they can intercept us."

He slammed open the door startling two maids charged with Gregor's care. Crossing the room in a pair of strides, Hurstwell scooped up Gregor and told the maids, "The castle is falling. Get to safety however you're able."

With that, he was out of the room and marching towards the passages that must lead to the docks. Thomas had seen Hurstwell focused and curt before, but this was different.

The sounds of the cannons and the shaking within the stones grew more pronounced, especially within the spiral stairs Hurstwell had led them to. Thomas had followed in silence and was just about to speak up when Hurstwell shoulder-crashed through a sturdy iron-reinforced door and outside. Overhead, a starry night was marred by twisting trails of smoke and the sounds of the waves lapping against the docks. The distant Valence Falls were drowned out by a few soldiers barking orders to the mass of people rushing onto the seven ships moored there. Three were caravels, and the other four small carracks. The Viceroy's personal fleet.

Over the din of the frenzied evacuation came the boasts of the cannons and the groans of the castle stones every time a shot found its mark. From the odd play of light on the water and the harsh odors in the air, Thomas knew a terrible fire had caught somewhere.

Someone dashing past clipped Thomas and sent him spiraling towards the dock's edge. He managed to grab a pier and hang on to keep from dropping into the frothing dark waters below.

Righting himself, he spotted Hurstwell looking back for him and nodding towards one of the caravels with gallant green sails trimmed with golden yellow and bearing the coat of arms of the Commonwealth. Its figurehead was of a hunter, bow drawn and the arrowpoint running along the bowsprit.

Thomas flung himself into the mass of people, some he knew and others he could only guess at, and wove his way to the ship. In the press of people and chaos, he lost sight of Hurstwell. By the time he reached the ship, another soldier was preparing to remove the gang plank.

"Wait! I need onboard that ship," he insisted.

The soldier stopped and gave him a shove backward. "That's the Viceroy's ship. No one else is allowed on."

Thomas stared desperately at the deck of the ship. Without Hurstwell or the others with him, he couldn't get on the ship or any ship, perhaps. After the grueling day and exertion, he was dirty and his clothes and hair a ragged mess. By appearance, no more than a commoner. A nobody.

"No, you don't understand," he protested and started to move for the boat.

He caught a right hook to his jaw and went down to the planks of the dock. The soldier shouted something at someone on the ship's deck before turning on Thomas, but at that moment, a thunderous crack echoed through the night air and a section of the castle came crashing down onto the end of docks. It smashed through, sending a tremor that took the soldier by Thomas off his feet.

Half stunned, Thomas saw the gangplank get knocked askew and knew it would slip away any minute and fall into the water. One of the other ships nearer the splintered section of dock began pulling away with its gangplank still crowded with people and supplies being loaded.

Something told him he had to move right now. Scrambling to his feet, jaw aching, Thomas dashed onto the gangplank. Every step sent a shudder through it and caused it to drift farther sideways. He knew he was racing against disaster and was still a good seven feet from the end when he felt the whole thing giving way and jumped for the ship.

On the voiceless utterances of his heart was a plea. The first such he remembered in his life.

High King help me!

Then he was leaping over the water as the boards he just been on splashed below. He was so close but he was already falling. He wasn't going to make it.

A strong hand reached from off the ship and grabbed his outstretched arm. The hold was ferocious and sent a jolt of pain from the sudden jerk of his fall being stopped. A little gasp escaped his lips before he frantically grabbed for the rescuer's arm with his other hand. He crashed into the curved side of the ship below deck level. The arm he clung to shuddered with the effort of holding him up.

Thomas held fast to his rescuer and fumbled to try to push off on the ship's side with his feet. He gained a slippery purchase that afforded him only a few inches of upward movement.

It was enough. The arm jerked back as he eased some of its load, and he grabbed hold of the bottom of the deck's railing. Helping hold himself up, he was hauled onto the boat a moment later.

He rolled onto the deck panting and saw his rescuer was Hurstwell, who was taking deep steadying breaths.

A few horrified people watched the chaos from the deck, but most were busying about making ready to sail.

Getting to his feet, Thomas took in the scene of the dock better now. Most of the ships were starting to cast off. Scores of people and supplies were still lined on the dock and up into exit points from the castle, trying to board any of the three ships that still had planks down. Above, the castle burned, and he saw the source of the chunk that had dropped onto the dock. Another enormous shard of castle stone hung precariously, ready to give any moment.

With a lurch, the ship under him began to move away from the dock. No sooner had it than the other portion of castle stone gave way and crashed into the sea beside the docks, sending an enormous wave at the fleeing ships. Two of the escaping carracks crashed into each other, and their impact sent the ship angling towards a stony outthrust of the castle that terminated in a defensive tower.

Hurstwell gripped his shoulder and cheered with fierce sincerity, "Courage, child. This isn't the end."

Their ship continued course toward certain shattering against the stone wall, making only the faintest noticeable adjustments away from it though Thomas could see the helmsman fighting the wheel with all he had to turn them.

Bracing himself, Thomas was dreadfully aware of every tremor in the ship as it scraped its hull along the wall, narrowly avoiding wrecking. As they reached clear waters, he spared a glance back. One of the carracks smashed disastrously into the tower. The damage looked worse the farther they went, and though the sounds grew faint, he heard them still in the recesses of his mind. Hurstwell was wrong; this was indeed the end. The end of the war, of the Restoration, and of any hope of seeing Ecthelowall's lands again.

12

Ll three ships that survived the crossing from Port Valence to Merlais docked in the early morning. Hurstwell came to rouse Thomas, but it wasn't necessary. Thomas was most certainly awake. He couldn't sleep at all. Memories of what he'd just seen wove into the tapestry of the vision he'd had and formed a terrifying tapestry he could not look away from. Nor could he explain it to Hurstwell. The old soldier had seen too much and was too much obliged to keep optimistic for such a conversation. The world was imploding, and Thomas couldn't imagine Hurstwell having ever tasted the desperation he felt for stability and safety to return.

The sky was pale rose and mostly cloudless. Surrounding the stern grey of Merlais's buildings—some of old Emeral style and some newer Ecthel constructions—were the distant green peaks and dales of the Tagel Mountains. Merlais's castle seemed to be situated precisely in the center of the scene and was by far the tallest structure with its thick, broad towers and round keep. Other than the emphasis on rounded structures, the city's architecture was not noteworthy. Though Thomas had heard that what New Ecthelowall's cities lacked in vibrance, its people more than compensated.

Assembled in wait on the docks of the sprawling harbor was an assemblage of dignitaries, most dressed in the light green and silver of Emeral though a few wore Ecthelowall's darker green and gold. The banners flown were primarily those of the Commonwealth, but old Emeralan ones were mixed in as well. There was certainly no deficit of pride and sense of identity among them.

"Stay close," Hurstwell instructed as he adjusted his hold on Gregor.

Thomas laid his head against Hurstwell's shoulder, earning him a grunt and a shove. It was the closest thing to humor Thomas could find, and was enough to get his legs moving when, after the dignitaries onboard his ship disembarked, it was their turn to walk down the planks.

Though he hadn't dared to believe it, he saw Viceroy Ecthelion at the head of a procession of officials striding forward to greet Baron Sornfold. A few steps back from the Viceroy were Delia and Mia. Despite himself, a flicker of hope kindled in his chest. If they had survived and the Viceroy had with all his stateliness and confident bearing, perhaps all wasn't so lost as he had imagined.

Even so, there was a contrast. Ecthelion was a tall, thin man with sharp features and hair that was going prematurely grey. Without his ceremonial armor and bold posture, he would not have looked a match for Baron Sornfold. The baron was a rotund man who did not bother with armor or arms outside battle. His posh outfit bespoke wealth and whispered of power. The kind achieved by investing resources wisely.

"Welcome, Honorable Viceroy Ecthelion. New Ecthelowall greets you warmly," Sornfold announced. Certainly, the Baron's boisterous tone and broad sweeping gestures made coming here feel far from desperation and more akin to a strategic withdrawal. Though Thomas couldn't help but notice even Mia flinched at him using the island's colonial name instead of the locally-preferred Emeral.

Whatever he lacked in couth, Baron Sornfold apparently did not suffer a lack of loyalty. Given only three of the seven ships belonging to the Viceroy arrived in port, it was doubtful that he hadn't already intuited what this meant. Two of the ships had scarring on the hulls, noticeable even in the early morning light. Their arrival was unannounced after a battle that should have kept the Viceroy busy on the main isle, pressing on towards Ecthalon.

No, Sornfold had to have guessed there was a major setback to the campaign. Perhaps he did not rightly estimate how bad, but he had to know that he had at hand an opportunity. The Viceroy's forces were coming looking tired, battered, and surrounded entirely by those loyal to the Baron. If he had wanted to get back in the Monarch's good graces, he need only to reach out and seize the Viceroy. But he didn't even seem to give a long enough pause to assess the matter before giving his joyful welcome. After which horns were blown, and the assemblage gave a bow.

Ecthelion seemed to recognize this. "Hale morning, faithful friend of the true Ecthelowall. We greet you in want of lodging on your fine shores and restore to you the daughters of your heart who were in our care."

"Viceroy, the hills of New Ecthelowall and the halls of Merlais are yours. Long may the Commonwealth endure," Baron Sornfold replied with a slight bow.

Before the Viceroy could offer the formal response of acceptance, Baron Sornfold spoke up again, this time bellowing to all present. "And for the auspicious return of my beloved daughters, we shall celebrate. A ball shall be held to commemorate their safe arrival on the shores of their birth."

Turning to the Viceroy, he said, "Now, let us retire to counsels peculiar to this hour."

Again, without receiving a response, the Baron turned and marched with his retinue back to Castle Merlais. "This isn't good," Thomas mumbled to Hurstwell.

"Why do you say that?" he asked as he carried Gregor up the winding stone way to the castle.

Thomas shot a glance askance at Hurstwell. "I'm no diplomat and not much of a student of court politics, but what just happened was a slight. Instead of deferring to the Viceroy, he took charge, treated Ecthelion as a subordinate. It muddies the waters on the Baron's allegiance."

Hurstwell huffed. "No, lad. He's made it abundantly clear to whom his allegiance belongs: himself."

Thomas's heart quickened its pace. That changed the tone of their arrival entirely. They weren't guests; they were prisoners.

13

The terrace overlooking the sprawling gardens of Merlais was lush in the summer afternoon's sun. Across it were dotted regal notes of purple heather and lilac in bloom. At the center of the gardens was a circular pool with mythic figures positioned at the four compass points, each posed with items identified with their legendarium. It was perhaps the most commonality the ancients of Emeral and Ecthelowall had. They both claimed to be descendants of Tislatna's exiles. Garcenilles, Surcalido, and Zilnen in the south claimed the same to a degree. It wasn't something many believed anymore. It existed in a still more nebulous space for most than did the Knights of Light.

Thomas stood straight after having spent almost an hour lost in thought looking out there. He chose the garden over the bustling city and harbor below or the decadent furnished rooms of the castle. He had long since decided that if he had to escape, it would be through the tall winding hedges and trees of this garden. He had mapped and re-mapped his course multiple times. There was no further indication the Baron would use them as a peace offering to the Monarchists. But then again, Thomas had been excluded from the important discourse of the past three days. He hadn't even been invited to the ball that evening. Not that he wanted to go. He didn't feel much inclined to celebrate, much less over the daughters of his would-be warden.

No, that wasn't fair. He was happy for them. They got back their home and family. It was only those refugees not of the Baron's household who faced an uncertain and likely lamentable fate.

"Thomas!"

Thomas whirled, cheeks reddened. Mia was standing a few feet away but had just yelled his name. Possibly from him not having responded to softer calls for his attention. The result was that she took in his discomposure and immediately donned a knowing smile.

"What were you up to?" She asked, tilting her head to look past him.

She was dressed once more in fine clothes, unmarred by the terrors of nights ago. Her hair was now in coppery curls that fell over her lightly freckled skin, which seemed to exude the same exuberant glow as the smile she wore. "Oh, uh, just getting lost in my thoughts," he answered with a shrug. How could he tell her he was dwelling on how they were doomed?

"Don't let your weighty thoughts pull you over the edge," she said with quiet sincerity.

An awkward silence descended as Thomas struggled to sort out the return of the winsome, earnest Mia from the glade days earlier. He found he had missed that Mia and that, above all else, felt strange amidst all his other discordant musings.

"You don't have to worry so much," she added after a moment. Again, oddly gentle. "Reinforcements have arrived every day since we got here."

"They have?" Thomas replied, hope surging within him. "I had seen a ship or two come into port with a few men but ..."

He trailed off as he realized from her surprised expression that those were the reinforcements she spoke about.

"Well, today's ship had many more than the others. In fact, you'll be pleased to know—"

"Pleased to know that I have arrived," Terrillian announced, strolling up to join them. He clasped Thomas on the shoulder and gave it a little shake. It seemed to refill some collapsed part of the teen.

"You're here! You survived the siege!"

The other teen was still in his silvery armor and seemed uninjured. He just shrugged as though it was nothing, but the set of his brow told Thomas that it was, in fact, remarkable. "The siege. The evacuation. The battle at sea."

Thomas took a moment to parse it all. "There was a battle at sea?"

Terrillian nodded. "Admiral Gelccer arrived about a day after you and the others got safely away. Fortunately, by then, the Sea Dragon showed up."

At this last bit, he smirked in a way that told Thomas he was missing some detail. "Captain Nerebold came?"

"Yes. Having known him under, um, humbler circumstances, I admit I took the tales that well-won him his sobriquet as exaggerations. We fought ship-to-ship in strikes and feints. His tactics turned the day from a crushing defeat to a strategic withdrawal. The grace of the High King was with us."

"Mhmm," Mia cleared her throat, returning Thomas's awestruck gaze to her. She had a quirk to her mouth that he knew meant she found something dubious. "Well, however you returned to us, we appreciate all you've done.

"If you'll both excuse me, I have to help Father prepare for the ball this evening. He has an important address to deliver and needs keen ears to help sharpen it."

Mia walked to the door back into the keep proper and stopped. She turned and seemed to be gnawing her lip. "Thomas," she began. "You weren't invited to the ball, were you?"

Thomas was unable to repress a chuckle. "Of course not."

"It begins just after sunset this evening. Come see me shortly before it begins. I'll be in the tower looking after Gregor for a bit."

Without waiting for his response, she nodded to the two guards at the doorway and ducked inside. Thomas let out a sigh when she was back inside. He immediately regretted it when he looked at Terrillian and saw the other with his eyebrows raised and smug grin fighting to break through.

"Stow away whatever nonsense you're thinking," Thomas snapped.

"As you like," Terrillian replied and looked out at the garden. He frowned.

"What's wrong?" Thomas asked, surprised by the quick shift in moods.

"That's awfully Tislatnean, isn't it?" he asked, gesturing towards the statues.

The disdain lacing the comment threw Thomas for a moment. He had been noting the same thing but with an appreciation for the legends. "It is, I suppose. Emeral, like Ecthelowall, claims deep roots back to the Lost Lands."

He pointed to one figure, a sensual woman with wild tresses clothed in heather, lilac, and ivy bearing a spear. "Ameralia, Princess of Tislatna and mother of Emeral, who colonized this island." Then he gestured to the figure on the opposite side, this one a powerful male wearing armor and lifting high a short sword. "This one you may appreciate more:

Cinaed, the Hero of Tislatna, who rescued the noble-hearted of Tislatna and with them founded Ecthelowall."

Terrillian turned to him, a brow raised in incredulity at best but looking close to disgust. Thomas quickly added, "Myths and legends from Tislatna's fall."

"A perversion of it," Terrillian amended. "I thought Tislatna's cults had been abandoned during the waning years of the Ancient Era, when Ecthelowall began pledging loyalty to the High King."

There was an accusation there, and it weighed heavily on Thomas's shoulders. All at once, he saw the statues through Terrillian's eyes and remembered his vision of the tower. Had he seen grotesque versions of these very figures among the clamoring throngs that snuffed out the light?

The young Knight's gaze softened, "Are you okay? You look ill."

Fighting to work moisture to his mouth, Thomas coughed and started to say, "Oh, just fine." Instead, he blurted out, "I saw something terrible."

Brows furrowed, Terrillian put a reassuring hand on his shoulder. "What did you see?"

Thomas wanted to run from the horrible reverie coming readily back to him, but Terrillian's gauntleted hand seemed to press down him with unyielding pressure. Stuck between the irresistible force of the vision and the immovable object of the armored hand, it spilled out. "I saw a tall tower with a marvelous light. It was warm and was the only luminance in the land as far could be seen. But its light grew fainter and fainter until these ... beasts ... came for it. They attacked the tower and tried to destroy it."

His voice hitched for a second and he saw Terrillian's dark eyes burn with interest. "Go on," he urged.

"And I hated it—I hated it with all in me. I knew the Tower

would fall. So, I ran over to stop the monsters. But it was no use. There were too many, and they were too strong, too vicious. Too much evil was against it.

"Just before the Tower fell, a brilliant light, far greater than the one that had been burning in the Tower, came down—maybe from the Tower, but it didn't seem that way—and it … obliterated all of it. Every dark thing. I felt like I could hardly bear it, and then I was back in the room I'd been in when it started."

For several seconds there was silence, and Thomas realized he was shaking. He fought to still himself and looked at Terrillian, who, by appearances, had gone through the ordeal as well. Somehow Thomas felt compelled to add, "The oddest thing about it was, even though I couldn't bear the light, I wanted it to come. I wanted it to rid the land of all the darkness."

All at once, Terrillian started chuckling. In little fits like it was meant to be kept in but couldn't be. Then he was outright laughing, and Thomas was worried for a moment that he had been a blathering fool just now, spouting visions about towers and monsters. Then Terrillian gripped Thomas in a tight embrace. "Of course, you wanted the light to prevail," he said. "Of course."

When Terrillian let him go, Thomas took a few steps back. "You don't think I'm going mad?" Though he now wondered about Terrillian.

"Not at all," Terrillian replied, calming some. "You've seen it. You've seen the Tower of Light."

"Is that a good thing?"

Bobbing his head to the side, Terrillian answered, "I'm not sure. It depends on how you feel about joining the High King's service and the Quest."

Thomas's chest tightened with dread and relaxed with wonder in alternation. "Woah, wait. What quest?"

"Remember when I told you that my friends and I were on a quest of great importance? And that I had left that quest to come here?"

"No," Thomas said with a shake of his head. But then something came back to him. A vague recollection from early in their meeting. "Well, maybe. That whole day was a bit much."

Nodding, Terrillian said, "That is fair. Perhaps I should take it slow. A friend of mine from my home in Black River, Caeserus, had a dream. A vision, like yours. It was of a tower that had a brilliant light atop it. Like yours, all manner of dark and devious creatures wanted to tear it down. They tried to, but four Knights rode out to its defense. In his dream, they helped keep the Tower alight."

A chill raced through Thomas. "That does sound very similar," was all he managed to say.

Shaking his head, Thomas tried to get a grip on himself. "But it's just a dream, not really a vision, right? Those don't really happen. And they aren't identical."

"Similar but not identical," Terrillian agreed. Then, almost ruefully, he added, "At one time, I called my friend's vision a 'silly dream,' and I was very much wrong. I cannot tell you what all of it means, only that you and Caeserus were not the only ones to have a vision about the Tower of Light. A Thane of Ordumair hundreds of years past saw something remarkably similar as well."

Once more, the chills returned and with greater force. They brought with them the ice of dread but receded to the burning fire of awe. "Really?"

"Mhm." Again, Terrillian placed his hand on Thomas's shoulder, but this time gently, without pressure. "You will have another vision soon. This time of the High King of All Realms.

When he comes to you, you will have two choices before you. Pledge yourself to him and join the Quest. Or reject him and stand amidst the sea of enemies within the darkness. There are only the two choices, and I cannot promise you safety and success in the Lowlands if you join the Quest. Only the promise that serving the High King is the right and good choice."

Thomas just stared at Terrillian for a long while, not speaking until the other let go and drew in a deep breath. He glanced down and smiled wryly. "I see you're bearing the spiritsword I gave you."

"Yes," he replied quietly. "I was looking at it when I had the vision ..."

Terillian's smile broadened. "As I would expect." Then he looked out over the garden and said, "I have to go to a meeting to plan our next moves. I'll see you at the banquet."

He took a few steps toward the door and spun around to say, "I wish you the best as you wrestle with the two great forces seeking you: the High King ... and Mia." He added the last with a wink.

"Ugh!" Thomas made as if he was going to chase Terrillian, but the other just laughed and ducked inside the keep. Leaving Thomas adrift. Aside from his nonsense teasing about Mia, Terrillian was right. Looking back out at the garden at the statues, he could feel it in his bones. There were two forces pulling at him. And his entire life he had been blind to both of them.

14

With some trepidation, Thomas climbed the final stairs to the tower in which Gregor was constantly attended. This was his first trip to see his cousin since arriving. It was doubtful whether he would have been admitted had he not been invited. Gregor's room was off-limits except to the physicians and those deemed important, which just underscored his internal struggles. All afternoon and well now into the evening, he had indeed grappled with what Terrillian had said. About the vision and the High King and a quest he had not sought. How could he be considered worthy of such an important quest but not enough to see a sick boy of his own blood?

Now standing a few feet from the room where Mia waited, he couldn't help thinking about Terrillian's other comments. The inane suggestion that he and Mia had something between them beyond a bizarre truce. His entire life stood in testament to the ridiculousness of that notion. All the same, here he was, feeling anxious going through the door ahead. On either side of it stood tall guards dressed in the colors of Emeral. Middle-aged and without marks of distinction on their tunics or armor. Meaning Gregor was important, but not THAT important to Baron Sornfold.

"Don't be a buffoon," he told himself and strode the last steps up to the door. He nodded to the guards stationed there and said, "Hale evening, I'm Thomas Fenwrest. Lady Mia summoned me."

As if to reinforce his incredulity, the guard raised a bushy brow after assessing him. His sense of duty won out, however, and he knocked on the door. From within, Mia's voice called out, "Yes?"

The guard opened the door partially, "Milady, Thomas Fenwrest wishes to see you."

"You may admit him," she replied.

Once the guard moved aside, Thomas stepped in, trying to analyze Mia's tone for clues to her feelings about him actually coming. He scanned the circular confines of the room. It was largely functional rather than stately, with a desk bearing remedies tried or to be tried. The only extravagance was the window looking out over Merlais's bay and the four-post bed upon which Gregor lay. Seated beside him, Thomas found Mia. She hadn't turned to him yet and was dabbing a wetted cloth on Gregor's brow. "You 'wish to see me,' hm?"

From how she accentuated the words with comical longing, Thomas felt even more foolish about Terrillian's words. "Not much else for me to do right now," he replied in his most nonchalant manner as he wandered over to her side.

"Oh, well, I apologize Emeral hasn't captivated you yet. Give it time," she replied, her voice soft and soothing. She continued gently dabbing it on Gregor's brow. "Mother always spoke of its power to capture the hearts of those who spend long enough on the isle. Her last wish when the fever took her was to travel once more from Yerst Castle back here."

"Merlais is charming, under different circumstances," he replied respectfully. It was rare for Mia to speak of her mother.

"Not Merlais per se," she said, putting down the rag into the wooden bowl of water on the floor beside her. "There are other places across the island she taught us about. Secret paths to vales and past the ruins of Old Emeral. Places that meant something to her but would not perhaps mean as much to others." She glanced up at him, eyes moistened. He could tell she was fighting tears, no doubt in part because she already had her makeup for the ball applied. But more so, he guessed, because it wouldn't do to show weakness in front of him.

When she looked down and took in a shaky breath, he questioned himself on that point. If she worried about looking weak, why confide about her mother's wishes at all? Particularly those from her mother's last precious days. "It sounds as though she knew Emeral's true beauty."

"Yes, she did," Mia agreed, her pleasure at his assessment rich in her choked voice though she seemed ready to start sobbing. He knew well how easily pleasant memories blended into the pain of the loss.

"Perhaps, you and Delia can visit those places while you are here," he said. "I've been told you have your mother's eyes, and through them, she'll see Emeral again." It was perhaps the most sentimental thing he had ever said.

She chuckled and stood finally to face him. "Are you feeling well? You've never been one for softheartedness."

"Oh, yes." Though for just a moment, he wasn't sure. Mia's red hair hung with its natural curls over her shoulders and down her back, unbraided or fettered. The effect was strange, much like how the faint darkening around her eyes accentuated the green, and the light freckles left exposed on her cheeks seemed to suit her far more than if they had been hidden. She was largely without makeup after all, and the better for it in his mind.

"What do you think?" Mia asked. She twirled, setting her green satin dress ruffles billowing, and the gold accents caught the sun through the window and gleamed. At the end, her eyes shone with the same tone and quality as the dress, aglow with expectation.

"You're beautiful. Radiant," Thomas had to admit. "I think this will be a night you'll always remember."

Her smile outshone every candle in the room. "I think so too. You ..." She paused, started to say something. Something weighty enough to part her lips to speak it, but so heavy she seemed unable to utter it.

"Yes?" Thomas prompted after a few seconds. For some reason, he very much wanted to hear what came next.

Mia's face fell, and she shook her head. "We should be going."

Suddenly Thomas felt incredibly anxious. He was in no way presentable beside her. He still wore the simple, rough tunic they'd brought him from barracks along with the dark trousers. And on this island, she was a Lady of Emeral, even if the lesser. He could not even be announced. It would be humiliating coming in alongside her. Or worse, having to watch her at the ball from the areas reserved for those of least standing. If she had not had such innocence about her offer as it lingered open in the air, he would have thought the cruel Mia had returned. "I, um, I think I'm actually due for a watch over Gregor. He is my blood, after all."

"Oh," was all she said, her face expression guarded.

Wincing, he reached for something to amend her seeming disappointment. "Perhaps, tomorrow, we could travel to see some of the sights your mother told you of? The two of us?"

Her eyes widened, and a thoughtful expression knitted her

brows before softening. "Yes, I would like that very much." She reached out then and gave his hand a light squeeze. Then she abruptly turned and hurried out the door, calling, "Goodnight," over her shoulder.

A guard shut the door after her leaving. Thomas exhaled slowly and turned his attention to Gregor. "Well, that was something, huh?"

As before, there was no sign of stirring from the boy. Rigid, pale, all but a corpse. For years Gregor had grated on Thomas's nerves, and he'd sometimes imagined violent means of bringing about comeuppance. But Thomas would never have wished such a horrible thing as this upon his cousin. Ironically, he only now wanted to help him and was equally powerless to aid as he had been to avenge himself.

Sighing, Thomas stretched and dropped onto the chair Mia had used. It was low, so it made his sword's hilt jab him. Thomas undid the strap holding the scabbard on and braced it against the wall nearest him. For several seconds he stared at it, thoughtful. He tapped his foot on the ground, over and over.

All at once he reached out and drew the sword, studying its myriads of etchings. Nothing of particular significance happened. The Ecthel lettering was familiar and readily understood. What he couldn't understand is how in Terrillian's hand he knew the spiritsword burned bright with that mystic fire, but try as he might, he could not will the same of the blade. Nor why on one night it induced a vision in him, and now it was merely a blade like any other.

Mia tried to deny it, but Thomas was fast growing to suspect that what he'd taken his whole life for myths might be so much more. They were stories, but stories that were truer than the reality he'd imagined he lived in. Deeper, more substantive.

As though sensing the intensity of his search, Thomas thought he saw a few letters glowing faintly. He read them,

> *"What no eye has seen,*
> *what no ear has heard,*
> *and what no human mind has conceived"—*
> *the things High King has prepared for those who*
> *love him—*
> *these are the things High King has revealed to us ..."*

Thomas huffed and looked out the window to the sprawling fuchsia sky overlooking the harbor as twilight raced to overtake the island. He could not fully articulate, even to himself, what the passage had induced, other than to say it was that now familiar weight, a heaviness heretofore indefinable. In this moment, he grasped it. It was a longing. Thomas was much like the island caught between the light and dark. And, though he might fight it, fated to fall deeper into the night.

Every fiber of his being rankled at the silent comparison. The inescapable gravity of it was the weight he felt. As though he were fighting from amidst quicksand to pull himself free. How he wanted to be! To see the fire, the light, to understand that peace Terrillian possessed. To look beyond what he now saw to that reality he could not conceive.

He glanced back down at the spiritsword, feeling silly that he was imagining the thing had grown warmer. Perhaps from his intensely tight grip on it. More words caught his eye.

"Everyone who calls on the name of the King shall be saved."

What was his name? How did one call?

On impulse, he stood and held out the spiritsword. "Please, majesty, show me your fire. I ..." He stammered, searching for what he wanted to say, but couldn't frame it. He settled on, "I want to understand."

Expectant, he watched the sword. For a moment, nothing happened. Then the sword suddenly began to glow, brighter and brighter, until Thomas had to shield his eyes. Even hiding them behind his arm, he perceived the room had been engulfed in the brightest light he'd ever seen. Warmth pressed on him from all sides.

A voice spoke to him, but it certainly was not Gregor's. It was too grave and regal, too soothing and compassionate to be his. The voice was a violent thunderstorm that could bring down trees and the softest of spring breezes in one. Thomas obeyed the instruction to lower his guard. And he saw he was in a light far brighter than he could understand and the one at the center of it, in fact its source, was the speaker. At once, though he'd never seen a single portrait to suggest it, he knew this was the High King of All Realms.

He dropped to his knees, his heart racing. "Forgive me, my King. I have no right to trouble you." Thomas had been around all manner of nobles since birth. Some were courteous and kind, some severe, and he'd more than once received a lashing and lectures for impropriety. None of them were a fraction as majestic as the High King. Thomas felt like his very seeing of the King's splendor was to profane it.

But the voice spoke again. Comforting words, which carried with them a stern adjuration to choose. Before him were two options. Yield and pledge fealty or return to the world as he knew it to face the fate he so feared. Not that fealty would lead to all ease and safety in the Lowlands, he was warned.

Bowing his head, Thomas had to rein himself in. Force himself to be thoughtful, purposeful, but he had already chosen, hadn't he? When he cried out, this was the very thing he wanted, needed. "I pledge fealty, Lord. I have no other Master than the High King of All Realms."

While his head was bowed, warmth pressed upon him. He kept his eyes shut, but he imagined tongues of flame coursing along his frame, working through his pores, burning through every sinew, racing through his blood, and arcing over his bones. It was the most wonderful and terrifying sensation of his life.

At last, the fire had finished its work, and the High King spoke to him again. Quick, simple instructions and a promise of the good to come.

Thomas opened his eyes, and he was standing there, the spiritsword held aloft, back in the tower with Gregor. So mundane after what he'd just witnessed. And yet, so much more than what he'd seen before. Everything seemed to have a new sort of contrast to it, as though he had only been seeing a fuzzy version of the world before. The most noticeable difference by far was the flames licking at the air from the length of the spiritsword in his hand.

15

With the flame's arrival, the weight from before was gone, burned away. Thomas drew in a breath and found the taste of it, the ease of it new as well. It was as if, to that point, he had been struggling to breathe and never noticed. Having known nothing but a strangled sip of the air, he now drank freely of it.

A whisper caught his ear. Before, he would have said it was the wind or his imagination. Having just experienced the vision, he recognized the voice. It was reminding him of his task.

Thomas looked over at Gregor and then at the spiritsword. He had been given instructions on what to do, the very kind that would make Mia question his sanity. "Let her," he told himself and strode back to his cousin's side. Gently, he obeyed the order and laid the blade's flat side against Gregor's chest.

Immediately, the flames caught on him, and Thomas feared he'd made some mistake. Misunderstood somehow. Yet he didn't retract the sword. He felt he mustn't. Not yet.

The flames traced the length of Gregor, and wherever they

touched, a purplish miasma was released and burned away. By the time they reached Gregor's face, Thomas could see the fire had also warmed and restored his color.

A moment later, Gregor stirred. His brow furrowed, and his lip curled in a sneer of fright. Thomas withdrew the sword and held up a hand placatively. The boy's eyes were opened to slits.

Thomas leaned forward and said, "Hey, can you hear me? Everything is all right. We're safe in Merlais."

Gregor set bolt upright and yelped, "No. We have to get out of here!"

"Woah, woah," Thomas soothed holding his hands up placatingly. "You don't have to worry. Like I said, we're all safe. We are on ..." He started to say Emeral but wondered if his younger cousin knew the name. "New Ecthelowall," he settled on. "Everyone is here and safe, including Viceroy Ecthelion."

"She's here?" Gregor replied, his eyes still wild with terror.

It took a couple seconds of pondering to guess who Gregor was referring to. With some chagrin, he nodded. "Yes, Delia is in the castle. Your bride-to-be is well. Far better than you were, in fact—"

"No, you blithering dolt!" Gregor screamed. "She is the one who poisoned me. She plans to betray us all!"

Thomas gaped. This had to be some sort of fever dream leftover from his poisoning. He was about to say such when a whisper pressed on his ear from where he couldn't discern. But he recognized the voice and the message. Gregor was telling the truth.

Dropping onto a stool and scooting closer to Gregor, he said in a low voice, "Everyone is going to a celebratory ball in this castle as we speak. Tell me everything."

Gregor shook his head vigorously. "We have to get out of here now. Everything is happening just as she said it would."

His eyes glanced out the window into the encroaching night. The calm of the bay below contrasted strangely with the anxiety lining his young face.

Catching his cousin as he tried to slip out of bed for the door, he gripped his shoulders. "No one is going anywhere until I have some answers. Mia, Hurstwell, and most of our nation's most important nobles are down there. Now speak, or I'll lay you back out."

The whisper was hot in his ears this time. That was a step beyond what was acceptable for him now. Biting his lip, Thomas exhaled some of his tension and said more gently, "Please, I have to know what we're facing."

To Thomas's surprise, the softer touch worked. Gregor stopped struggling, and some clarity returned to his expression. He gave a little wobble that Thomas took for a nod. "Okay?" Thomas said. "So, what's all this about Delia betraying us?"

"I do not know why she is doing it," Gregor mewled pitifully. "When those strange stiff-walkers attacked, she acted afraid until Hurstwell was knocked out. I may have, um, shrieked at that moment. But she just relaxed and smiled at me."

He shuddered and looked back at the window again. "I told her we had to run, and she just giggled. She said there was no running. Everything was happening as intended. On the ride in the carriage, she stabbed my palm with the tip of a dagger. There was a little bit of some kind of poison on it. That is when she told me that soon we would all be here on Emeral, and then the Monarch's forces would crush the Restoration with one stroke."

Had the whispered council of the High King, so fresh and fierce as it was to him, not told Thomas to trust Gregor, he would have ignored all of it. That Delia could betray them all was unthinkable. But so was the fiery blade he held and the reality of the One True King of All Realms.

Finding it difficult to compose the words, Thomas swallowed hard and mumbled, "Come with me. I'll need your testimony to convince the others."

"Not a chance! There is nothing that could make me—"

The door to the room was flung open and crashed against the stone wall with wooden cry of shock. As Thomas whirled back from it, instinctively raising his spiritsword to a guard, three soldiers in Emeralan distinctive light green entered. They, too, had swords drawn.

The lead soldier announced, "You both are to come with us. Lady Delia has commanded that you are to be kept under lock until the evening's events are concluded."

Such a flower of speech for the base and fetid meaning to it all. Gregor was right. Those guards had overheard them, and now they would capture or kill them to keep the secret hid.

"You have no right to hold us," Thomas countered. Buying some time to better position himself between the soldiers and Gregor who had groaned piteously at the sight of them. "We are guests of Viceroy Ecthelion, his word supersedes the Lady's."

"Not on the Isle of Emeral," one of the others replied with a snicker.

"Lay down your arms," the lead intoned. "Now."

"A hale evening, ever before the dawn of Ecthelowall's Commonwealth," Thomas recited.

"Take him. Capture the child if you can. The Lady wants him for spectacle," the captain instructed.

Thomas did not wait for the two at back to fan out to encircle them. He struck first, launching a sortie that forced back the first soldier and pushed the other two into the hall beyond. Their only hope was to keep those trained warriors of Emeral from using their numbers against Thomas.

The lead Emeralan was only set off foot for an instant, before snapping his long rapier around in a counterattack. Thomas found his blade ready for the block faster than he thought himself capable. His attacker seemed surprised as well, allowing Thomas to seize the offensive again and, in three quick strikes, disarm the other man.

Backing away, rubbing his singed hand, the Emeralan looked to his two subordinates. One charged forward with a messy killing swipe leveled at Thomas's head.

Sidestepping, Thomas came around and sliced across his foes' back as he stumbled past. It was a grazing blow, but the fiery spiritsword's touch left a searing mark, and the Emeralan dropped to the ground with a wail.

Thomas felt sorry for him for an instant, but didn't have time to dwell as the remaining armed aggressor charged, forcing him into a hasty block. Thomas struggled to keep his footing. This soldier was bigger than him by six inches and at least fifty pounds.

The man must have realized that as well and leaned into his attack. Pressing down, Thomas's arms started to shake under the strain. He couldn't bear up under this much longer, especially with his balance as precarious as it was already. Muscles burned in his legs, his arms, and he knew he was going to fall. Once he did, he wouldn't be getting back up. This Emeralan would see to it.

High King, help me, please! I cannot stand alone.

The spiritsword in Thomas's hands flared brighter, and Thomas felt strength coursing into his limbs. He wasn't just holding his own; he began to push the man off, to the other's horror. Once braced for it, he broke the lock between the blades, struck left, right, ducked a desperate strike, and felled his foe in one more move.

Looking up, he saw the first Emeralan had already fled. That would mean trouble soon. Thomas took in the two men he had defeated, both writhing on the ground with tendrils of smoke roiling from their wounds. He didn't imagine either to be fatal and couldn't bring himself to think at that moment about what he would feel or do if it came to the point of killing an Emeralan.

"Come on," he called to Gregor. "We have to warn the others."

The boy had watched it all with eyes wide, and he recoiled from Thomas. Sighing, Thomas reached out and grabbed his cousin's hand and yanked him off the bed he was crouched on. "I'm not going to hurt you," he insisted.

"Father would have you flayed if you even tried to," Gregor insisted as he dropped to the floor and struggled against Thomas's grip on him.

Not letting up, Thomas hauled his cousin out of the room and into the hall. As he did, he ground out, "I helped free you from the poison and fought off those fiends who wanted you dead just now, didn't I?"

"So it seemed," Gregor replied, still working at getting free. "But—"

"No. There is no 'but' here. We don't have time for silliness. If you aren't just spouting fever-dream nonsense, then we have to warn everyone or the Viceroy, Mia, your father, and everyone who stood against the Monarch, including us, will be killed. And not quickly. We will be made examples, do you understand?"

"Yes, sir," Gregor said, a quaver in his voice.

Finally, he stopped trying to slip free. It was the first time he had spoken to Thomas deferentially. It felt so strange that

Thomas didn't even bother responding. He just nodded and led the way to the large, centrally located room where he knew the ball was taking place.

They ran down several flights of stairs through myriad passages. Thomas rounded the turn, all but dragging Gregor. Charging ahead, they reached the hall leading to the ballroom. From beyond the closed doors drifted the notes of a sweeping concert piece being played on violins. By appearances, there were only two guards present, both Emeralans.

Glancing back the way they came to check for pursuers and finding none, he took a deep breath. "Gregor," he said, summoning his younger cousin's attention as the other huffed from the exertion.

As soon as Gregor tilted his head up to regard him, Thomas began under his breath, "Don't panic. I'm going to try to get us in. If I can't without a fight, I'll distract the guards, and you run in. Find Viceroy Ecthelion—"

"The Viceroy?" Gregor wheezed incredulously. "I have never met him!"

"Fine, then find ... Mia." Though he knew she would be the hardest to convince of danger from her sister. If the fiery sword in his hand didn't seem to burn hotter at the very thought of Delia, he wouldn't be able to believe it either.

"That is as fool a plan as I have ever heard!" Gregor grumbled too loud.

"Hey, you there with the sword! Lower your weapon and state your business," one of the guards called out.

Thomas gnawed on his bottom lip and decided there was no turning back. "Fool or not, that is our road now."

The guards were halfway down the hall to them. Only one guard had his weapon drawn. "Help us, High King," he murmured under his breath. The whispered guidance came to him almost immediately.

Thomas walked seven deliberate strides forward and then broke into a sprint, dropped his shoulder, and plowed into the unarmed guard. That guard wasn't much older than him and about the same build. Pain radiated from where his shoulder impacted the man's ceremonial leather armor, but the guard went down, and Thomas was still on his feet and turning to the other guard before the older, burlier man could react. With a deft strike, he knocked aside the man's sword and slammed him into the wall with his forearm pressed to his throat. "Now!" Thomas bellowed, not daring to take his eyes off the older soldier he had pinned.

Out of the corner of his eye, he saw Gregor stumbling past at a caper, trepidation at what was ahead only slightly outmatched by his apparent fear of Thomas at that moment.

The boy had scarcely snuck into the ballroom when the first guard got back to his feet and grabbed Thomas, slinging him off the older one.

Taking the moment and dashing a few extra steps down the hall, Thomas spun around to face his attackers. To his horror, the younger one spun and took off into the ballroom after Gregor. The older one, meanwhile, rubbed his throat and glowered.

Throwing a feint at the guard, Thomas wheeled around to make a break for the doors, but the older man didn't take the bait. He shifted with surprising speed for his size and the age his graying hair betrayed. The old guard swung at Thomas and it was all the teen could do to get his block up in time. He hadn't properly braced himself and stumbled backward.

"I don't know who you are, Ecthel," the old guard grumbled. "But I'm going to enjoy dragging you in irons to the dungeon."

"If you truly care about Emeral then you will let me through."

"Is that so?" he challenged and swung to force Thomas back toward the right wall, trying to pin him there.

"Truly," Thomas said, narrowly skirting the trap and opting to back farther away. He could hear the clomp of many heavy footfalls coming toward them. More guards were coming. How they already knew to come was immaterial at this point. The simple truth was he was out of time.

The other man seemed to realize that and stood in the middle of the hall. All he had to do was hold Thomas at bay until the reinforcements caught up.

"In the name of the High King, move!" Thomas pleaded.

The old soldier grunted. "What are you invoking mystic rubbish for, whelp?" the guard snapped.

"I had hoped you were honorable," Thomas countered, though without petulance.

"You snipe," the guard spat, "For that, I'll finish you now!" And charged.

Thomas had a half second to react and dodged left as the other hacked down the middle. Taking the opening, Thomas sliced across the man's hands. The guard dropped his sword with a tinny clang and tucked each hand under the opposite arm, more burned than cut. Curses flew from his lips.

Thomas slipped past and dashed into the ballroom expecting to have to struggle to find Gregor in the midst of a sea of extravagant poofy dresses and suits. But when he entered the room, it was silent. What faint strains of music had reached his ears before had died. Everyone looked at the center of the dance floor where Delia stood, gripping a dagger planted in her father's back.

16

Thomas gaped, his muscles frozen by the same chill that threatened to ice his blood. Someone cried out, maybe Mia. He didn't turn his head to look. There was no looking away from what he saw. Delia was near enough that he could see the quiet fury in her face as she twisted the dagger and jerked it back out. Till this moment, Gregor's accusations had felt abstract. He believed them, but this was something wholly other. A nightmare come to life.

Baron Sornfold collapsed to his knees, one hand bracing himself up, the other futilely reaching back towards the wound. Delia loomed over him. Garbed in a form-fitting dress of green with a silver drape and luxurious jewelry dangling from her neck and wrists, she hardly seemed a potential assassin. Yet her once strikingly beautiful face was filled with a cruelty so intense it kept Thomas frozen in place even as she lifted a lithe leg and kicked the Baron, sending him onto his back with a sharp groan.

By now, Mia was in view, Gregor clinging to her lovely

101

dress in a futile attempt to hold her back. "Deli!" Her voice was hoarse with shock and bewilderment. "What are you doing?"

With all the cool ease of a viper slithering off from its victim, Delia drifted to her sister's side, the dagger pointed casually towards her, but not in an actively threatening way. "I'm giving him what he wants, sister ... and taking it away in one stroke."

The Baron groaned again and convulsed on the ground, his body twisting from an unseeable agony. Mia started toward him, but Delia held out the dagger to bar her. "The poison on the dagger mimics the symptoms of mother's illness."

"Why would you do this? Mother died of Riodelta Fever, not poison."

"Perhaps," Delia replied as if it were a tiny detail. "But it was his corrupt glory-seeking that brought the illness to her. And to Mark.

"Though for the latter, I will have to thank him. If I had married Mark, I would have forever remained a happy little piece in his power games. It is through losing Mark that I met Maldes and obtained the means of unshackling Emeral forever."

With that, she sheathed her dagger into the innocuous slip of fabric on the dress from whence it came and clapped her hands together. The bewitched horror holding the room broke, and several nobles of the Restoration crossed onto the dance floor to apprehend her. They were stopped as from all four entrances came guards and soldiers wearing the colors of Emeral and bearing standards of the Monarch.

Mia brought a hand to her mouth as the guards methodically encircled those gathered, whom Thomas realized too late were all loyalists to the Viceroy. Including Ecthelion, who was grabbed by either arm and brought to the center of the room. Thomas felt a brusque bump from behind, pushed towards the room's middle as well.

He tried to maneuver to the edge of the dance floor near enough that he could get to Mia and Gregor if possible. So far, no one had noticed his spiritsword.

This close, he could see tears streaming down Mia's cheeks. "But I don't understand. How could you betray us all to death and servitude to the Monarch? How is Emeral any freer under the tyrant of Ecthelowall than the tolerant Viceroy?"

A scowl descended on Delia's face as the unmistakable notes of anger and accusation drifted into Mia's words. "I shouldn't expect a silly little girl still wound tight around father's little finger to comprehend this. Father hadn't tried to use you as a bargaining token in his self-serving schemes yet. Do you know he had me betrothed to that disgusting little grub hanging off your dress within a day of Mark's death? He happily played dollies with me and could've cared less if I spent the entirety of my life in misery under that little beast's thumb."

Until he saw it burning in her gaze, Thomas would never have imagined Delia capable of such fury.

"But Maldes was different. He understood my predicament. Even sympathized in his own way. And so, he proposed an arrangement. In exchange for Emeral's loyalty, he has made it a protectorate under my care. No longer the New Ecthelowall those usurpers tried to make it. No longer ruled from Yerst Castle. Free to govern its magnificent destiny as it was always meant to."

"Until Maldes's successor chooses to burn down all your ambitions!" Mia stated with a melancholy sort of humor. Thomas was afraid she might go into shock.

A smile more serpentine than Thomas would have expected from Delia formed on her lips. "Didn't I say father got what he wanted? I'm betrothed again, to Maldes Ilyron, the only rightful claimant to the Monarch throne. And the child I bear will reign over both Ecthelowall and Emeral, with the heart and blood of an Emeralan."

She glanced over to the now still form of Baron Sornfold. "Just the sort of match he salivated over. But none of the rewards will be in his fat fingers."

This last she said quietly, much of the menace and venom draining from her tone, as if eulogizing him. Or, more likely, savoring the culmination of her revenge.

Mia exhaled shakily and drew herself up. "You know, I pity you, Delia. Your grief and father's selfishness led you to become the very thing you abhor. A piece in a game you cannot control. Even if you did choose a few of your moves."

Delia huffed. "You seem to have chosen your move as well. As your Queen, such impertinence is a punishable offense."

To the guards all around the room, she ordered, "Take them, alive or dead, to the dungeon. We will accord justice to each once my betrothed arrives. Make sure Ecthelion lives, however. I'm sure Maldes will wish to savor his own small retribution on the Viceroy." With that, she smoothed her dress and began walking towards the edge of the circle where several guards had made an exit for her. As soon as she left the room, there was an easing of pent-up tension. It was like a blanket being lifted away and finding one's self able to breathe freely again, but it also was like losing a catapult's pin. All around the room, Loyalists and Monarchists sprang to fight as the unarmed nobles and ladies dashed to the center of the room in desperate pursuit of safety.

At Thomas's left, a Loyalist soldier fell with a cry. The Emeralan Monarchist tried to swipe at Thomas as well but over-extended, and Thomas was able to dodge the attack and leave a burning strike across his steely cuirass.

As the Monarchist reeled backward, Thomas heard a whispered warning and dropped to the floor as a crossbow bolt shot through the air above him. Even before arrows and bolts started flying, the battle was destined to be a slaughter. No one, save a handful of honor guards and Thomas, had been armed. It wouldn't last much longer. He had to get Mia and Gregor out of here.

Crawling towards the center of the room, he spotted them. The former was sheltering the terrified boy as she scanned the room. Desperation etched into her brows. That's when Thomas spotted a crossbowman taking aim at them. "Mia!" He scrambled to his feet and leaped to push her out of the bolt's intended path. He crashed into her dragging her and Gregor to the floor. He had anticipated the pain of the bolt at least grazing him but felt nothing. Looking up, he saw the crossbowman crumple to the floor. From a side entrance, Terrillian emerged with a group of five or so others. For several seconds he sat there in awe of how Terrillian's cuirass, pauldrons, and every bit of his armor burned with the same marvelous fire. Had it always been this bright, and Thomas just couldn't see until now?

Terrillian and the other new arrivals battled their way across the room. To Thomas's dismay, there didn't seem to be any additional reinforcements coming.

"Get off us, you brute!" Mia yelled. As Thomas rolled to the side, he saw her expression turn to surprise. "Thomas."

He nodded. "I decided to come after all," he joked weakly.

She rolled her eyes but laughed through building tears. "You saw ...?"

"Yes. I tried to get Gregor through the guards to warn you and the others. I'm so sorry we were too late."

Mia looked away toward where her father still lay and then

grabbed Thomas's arm. "They're trying to take away the Viceroy!"

Scrambling to his feet, he charged after the trio of Emeralan soldiers who were attempting to carry off the Viceroy. Ecthelion looked conscious but limp, offering no resistance.

Thomas dove, tackled the rear most soldier, and managed to tumble on top of him. Getting to his feet, he used the pommel of his spiritsword to render the man unconscious.

The other two soldiers glanced at one another uncertainly, each holding the Viceroy under the arms. Up close, Thomas could tell Ecthelion wasn't injured physically. His eyes were distant and unattached to what was unfolding around him for some other cause that Thomas could only guess. Perhaps they had poisoned him too.

Before the pair holding him could sort out the situation, he charged forward and left burning slashes across them both. They dropped the Viceroy clutching their searing wounds.

Thomas heard an awful, meaty "thuk" sound and gaped at the bolt that had just struck the Viceroy below his right collarbone. The next moment, pain exploded in Thomas's left arm. He spared a moment to examine the jagged tear the bolt had left on the way to its mark.

Dropping down and gritting his teeth against the pain he tried to talk to the Viceroy who seemed to barely register what had happened. "I'm going to get you out of here, sir. Please, if you can, help me."

Thomas grabbed one of the Viceroy's arms and hooked it around his neck, intending to help him hobble to the same doors the Emeralan soldiers had intended to use.

Ecthelion finally stirred. "No, lad. The other direction. That will take us to the castle courtyard. We must head to the south entry. That will lead us to the gardens." He suddenly sucked a sharp breath as the pain finally hit him. Through his teeth, he added, "Less likely to be well-guarded."

"Yes, sir," Thomas replied, relieved to feel the other bearing more of his own weight and returning from whatever foggy lands his mind had passed through.

The relief died quickly as Thomas realized the south entrance was blocked by several soldiers who were finishing off the remaining Loyalists. Angling them toward the entrance Terrillian and the others came through, Thomas said, "New plan. We worry about getting out first. Then what's beyond next."

"Sir Hurstwell's tutelage is evident in you," Ecthelion commented somewhat dryly.

Hurstwell!

Thomas hadn't even thought about his old mentor. On impulse, he stumbled to a halt and began scanning the room for him. He didn't see the grizzled Knight anywhere.

Ecthelion tugged on Thomas, forcing him forward. "If we stop, we are both finished."

"But Sir Hurstwell ..."

Ecthelion didn't stop but lost a half step. "I do not know, child. He was assigned to the port this evening. Another ship load of Loyalist refugees was expected."

Thomas felt himself grow wobbly, and his knees almost gave way. The Viceroy strained to hold him up now, and Thomas heard the faint cry of pain he gave for the trouble.

The whisper of direction came to him and seemed to bolster his legs. He pushed on, this time much faster. They had to get out, or all this chaos and loss would be for nothing.

By now, the room was shifting. The Loyalists were all collapsing towards the exit Thomas sought. He and Ecthelion managed to skirt behind the lines, and as they did, Terrillian gave a whistle. Almost the whole defense collapsed backward around the Viceroy and Thomas.

To his relief, the next sound Thomas heard was Mia's voice. "Here, let me help." She worked around under the Viceroy's injured arm and helped support it. The nobleman winced but said, "Thank you dearly."

In unison, the group backed toward the door before Terrillian yelled, "Now!"

All at once, everyone turned to run out into the Eastern corridor.

As they ran, bolts and arrows clicked off the stones at their backs as they took a series of twists and turns. Thomas didn't look back to verify, but he knew some fell behind.

"Wait, where are you leading us?" Mia said. "This leads out to the gardens."

Thomas was surprised the group had managed to find a way to double back to that route. "Isn't that the safest place to go?" Thomas asked and eyed the Viceroy.

"No! We're totally exposed there. Follow me. I know the way to a secret exit."

Thomas thought for a moment about the odds that the soldiers also knew of the exit but decided it didn't matter at this point. "We're with you, Lady Mia," the Viceroy answered for them all.

Some of the group did not hear the change and careened off in the opposite direction at the next juncture. Thomas did spare a glance to see that at the least they had Terrillian and two other Loyalists to their backs, and running a few paces ahead, continually checking back with Mia, were two more soldiers and one lesser nobleman Thomas couldn't place. Possibly the last patron of the Restoration from the South left alive.

Rounding a sharp turn, Thomas barely had time to realize

they were entering the bottom of a tower. As soon as everyone was in, Mia instructed, "Bar the door!"

Two soldiers saw to it and as they did, she addressed the group in hushed tones. "I'm about to open a secret passage out onto the moors. There's an old path through Tagel Mountains past the ruins of Old Emeral that leads to Darby Downs. If we can get there, I might be able to rally enough supporters who haven't yet joined the conspiracy to make a stand."

"I like your plan, but I have a better option than making a stand. We make for the coast and find a vessel to get us back to Libertias," Terrillian advised. "Libertias should grant you all asylum, and doesn't risk handing the Viceroy over to officials in Darby Downs who may already be part of this conspiracy."

"I seriously doubt my sister managed to sway the whole island to her side without me knowing it. I have friends and correspondents in Darby Downs. Surely they would have told me as much."

Panting a bit as he did so, Ecthelion spoke up. "Let us take the path you proposed. Should we make it to Darby Downs outskirts unassailed, then we shall evaluate our options fully. I was wisely counseled that we are in a position now of having to take the open doors before us and consider what lies beyond after we cross that threshold." Having said this, he patted Thomas on the back.

Mia noticed and raised an eyebrow. She started to say something and then scowled. "Very well. When we go out, we should be in the shadows of a castle wall till we reach the wood line. From there, I'll show you the paths my mother taught me."

She glanced at Thomas, her expression tight with barely restrained sorrow. Mia suddenly added, "All of you flaming sword wielders should sheath them. Our only advantage till we're on the wild paths is stealth."

At this, she glanced down at Thomas's spiritsword and

then up at him with a curious question in her vivid emerald eyes. In the light of the sword's flames, the streaks from her tears stood out sharper on her face. It was all he could do to concentrate on sheathing the blade while still supporting the Viceroy. It struck Thomas then that Mia, for once, had seen the flames of a spiritsword. On his, in fact. There was no time to sort through that, though as she was already pushing open a door that had been masterfully blended into the rest of the wall.

Moments later, they were all in the salty night air of Merlais and swathed in a deep dark. Thomas could see that Terrillian had borrowed a cloak for his armor, but even with it, there was a faint glow around him.

Somehow Thomas doubted their foes would spot them all the same. No windows looked out from the tower until much higher up, and its curvature blocked view of this parcel of land between the castle and the wood. By the time they were viewable from the tower, they would be deep among the trees.

As the thick dark branches enclosed them, Thomas tried to focus on the path ahead and properly supporting the Viceroy. He did not want to think about how their plight was still more desperate than before. Was there any haven for them left in the Lowlands?

Dropping to the ground with a thud, Thomas grimaced. The jolt radiated aches throughout him that set his teeth on edge. He resisted the urge to check the field dressing. Thinking about Mark and how he succumbed to the infection in his battle wound was unavoidable. It helped to remind himself that the Viceroy really had the worst of it and was holding himself together. What's more, they were supposed to be resting, but Thomas was pretty sure he would never escape the restlessness he felt living on the run.

"Dubh berries?" he held out the dark juicy clusters to Mia.

"Thank you," she replied quietly and took several. She handed three to Gregor, who greedily devoured them.

At the end of them, a bit of juice dribbling down his chin, he finally remembered himself and returned his thanks.

To his left, Terrillian sat down with a long sigh. He popped a couple of berries he'd foraged into his mouth. "Mm, now this reminds me of my trip to Ordumair."

Thomas focused on the fire crackling and popping before him. Three days slinking through the wilderness to reach this halfway point. Glancing up the slope, he could see the jagged outline of Old Emeral's ruins in the cool moonlight. A dozen buildings, one particularly large, sprang up on the slopes of the hills. Their shapes were largely reminiscent of the same rounded architecture he had seen in Merlais, save for the gaping holes, sunken roofs, and preternatural quiet that hung over them. Even tombs seemed better places to lodge near. At least they didn't reek of emptiness and abandon.

"That was once a palace," Mia commented. "Mother told me all that remains are the skeleton of it. At one time, more than a thousand people worked the land, cared for their families, and crafted songs that still echo into the moors."

Thomas turned his attention to her. "I could use a song right now. Do you know any?"

"Um, well, one. My mother sang it ... um, about my father."

"Oh."

There was a chuckle beside him, and Terrillian, between bites of his berries, said, "You know we would all like to hear that. I bet Thomas would especially." He elbowed him in the side.

Mia gave a flicker of a smile, and then her brows knit for an instant as she began humming a tune. After a few seconds, she began her mother's song:

> *"I climbed Tagel mountain,*
> *For want of view,*
> *Bounding like a fountain,*
> *There I found you.*
>
> *I passed a vale wide,*
> *Sure my heart knew,*
> *No moor could such good hide.*

I forded a wild stream,
Loneliness slew,
Daring to trust what seem.

Bold before a blue sky,
Long I have wondered why,
By such meet I was tie,
For no price will I lie,

There I found you,
A bond so true,
No ill can hew,
There I loved you."

By the time she finished, Mia was in tears. Her cheeks stoked hot and red. Getting to her feet, she shook her head. "I'm sorry," she said and dashed off toward the ruins.

Thomas watched Mia go and resisted the immediate impulse to get up and follow her. The whole group sat in silence for several minutes; the fire's crackling and the distant hooting of an owl and chirp of insects filled the void.

Watching the flames flicker for as long as he could stand, he got to his feet and knocked off the bits of dirt from sitting on the ground, and marched off after her. It was chillier away from the fire, and as he wound up the half-sunken stairs from the lower city to upper, gooseflesh rose on his arms. Passing by the darkened husks of what had been the original capital of Emeral, each structure destroyed during the conquest of Emeral by Ecthelowall was a silent accusation. He had never questioned the right of Ecthelowall to claim the near isle until now.

He could add that to a thousand other questions and emotions that couldn't be sorted for the moment. Maybe he never would, regardless of how long after this he lived. Which, for the moment, wasn't looking to be very long.

A bit of broken stone he'd unwittingly kicked skittered across the overgrown street and clacked off a pile of building rubble. There was a flicker of motion higher up at the pinnacle of the ruins. In the moonlight, he caught a glimpse of Mia. She peered down from atop one of the buildings.

"Hey, don't worry, it's just me. Thomas," he called to her in hushed tones. Whether the urge for quiet was from fear of pursuers or reverence for those who died here, he couldn't say.

Mia didn't answer him. She just stood still in the darkness, her one luxurious dress damp and damaged, though the gold of her dress shone in the moonlight, as did the richest copper streaks in her hair. But something about her posture, her subdued mannerisms after having been torn through with sorrow so recently felt off.

Scrambling up the rest of the way to the top level, he realized they were on the summit of the mountain the city had been built on. Mia was standing some fifteen feet higher, having climbed on top of the building that had been a motte or temple or some other key structure before its abandonment. He called again, "Mia?"

There was no answer. Looking for a way up, he noticed the damage to the structure had made unstable rubble stairs. Its grit and slippery moss-covered surface were unpleasant under his sore hands and feet, but he managed to get up, even with his injured arm protesting. Standing on top of the building, he finally had the right angle to perceive that Mia on a section of the building that wasn't well supported and overlooked a sharp drop-off to a particularly jagged swath of destruction below. One wrong move, and there would be no recovering from the fall.

"Mia, be careful. The roof isn't supported there."

"Brilliant observation," she replied but without any bite. It was as if an echo had reached him instead of her live words.

"You would expect nothing less of me, right?" he said, trying to sort out where he could stand without endangering them. He had to settle for a few feet behind her.

She glanced over her shoulder. "Go away, Thomas."

The expressionless demand and slackness of her face scared him more than their perch. He dared another step closer to her. "Ah, I will be happy to give you some space, once we're back at the campsite."

"I'm not going back to the camp. I'm not going anywhere ..."

He swallowed back his anxiety and dared another step. It was so dark, even with the moonlight, he almost stumbled into her thinking his foot was on the stone sooner than it was. His noisy misstep caused her to whirl around. She looked like a feline tensed to pounce or flee. Neither would end well for them.

"Sorry, I'm not as familiar with this place as you are."

"Of course, you're not. You're an Ecthel."

That was a strange barb. Was she drifting into the same vein of thinking as her sister? What was he supposed to say? He settled on, "Not all of us can have as rich a heritage as you."

Her scowl at the pandering was furious. "Rich heritage? My mother's people were ruined by my father's. My father killed my mother with a disease he brought back to her, and my sister killed him for it. Now I'm on the run from her with the heirs of an empire that destroyed the buildings we stand among. That crushed the life out of the people who built them."

Facing away from the moonlight, her face was swathed in shadows, but Thomas found he could still see her impassive expression clearly as she swiped away an errant tear. She stamped her foot, sending a little cascade of stone fragments tumbling below, and his heart stuttered. "I have lost everything. Even the memories of my parents, my life is tarnished now."

"I'm so sorry," Thomas said, this time not having to manufacture the emotion of the words. "I know how badly it hurts."

"How could you?" She snapped and stepped towards him, giving him a shove. "How could you know what this feels like?"

Anger and fear at the danger she was putting them in welled up. "Because I've dealt with that feeling for years, you selfish brat."

The shock on her face was immediate and she gave him a hard slap. Staring at her, ready to land his own blows, his hand grazed his spiritsword's hilt and the heat from touching it seared through him, jerking him out of his wounded stupor. The rawness of his anger and pain lingered there, sharply focused by the sting in his cheek. For just a moment though, he could see through it, beyond it. Maybe for the first time in his life.

He hadn't been in service of the High King long, and it had been a rocky journey thus far, but he was sure this hate, and there was no other word for it, couldn't be something he wished Thomas to cling to. Certainly not in this moment when it clearly endangered both his own and Mia's safety.

Unconsciously, as if to test his rightness, he brushed his hand back over the pommel of the spiritsword. It did not burn him this time. In fact, he gripped the hilt, and a wave of calm and peace cut through the thick turmoil in his chest. He drew in a steadying breath. His head cleared.

Mia's eyes fixed on his hand on the sword hilt and widened with accusation. She reared back, her fist balled, ready to defend herself.

"No, no!" he said and just managed to catch her wrist

before she could hit him. She struggled to get free, yelling curses at him. Grabbing and holding her tight against him was the only thing he could think of to keep them both from falling to their deaths. He shushed and soothed and eventually found himself rubbing her back in soothing circles.

At length, her struggling ceased, and he felt her taking deep breaths between the shuddering sobs she buried in his chest. After several seconds, he said, "I am not going to hurt you. Not by intention."

"Why not? A selfish brat like me? Half-Emeralan. Why not just finish me and end my misery?"

"You're not a selfish brat ...not really. And you aren't the only one who has felt like they have nothing left. Do you think it's easy knowing your father destroyed his family's legacy and then killed himself to hide from the shame?"

Feeling some of the tension drop from her body, he gave her space to push back enough to look up at him. Her expression was unreadable, "I thought the castle fire was an accident."

He shrugged and drew in a breath. "That's what my uncle told everyone, but I know better. Your parents made mistakes, but at least by all accounts they genuinely loved each other. I can't say I've ever seen love except between strangers. All I have left of my family is the memory that my parents thought death was better than a less extravagant life with me."

It was the first time he had admitted those things openly to himself, let alone anyone else. It was all he could do to keep the tears back and to keep from dropping to the ground. After a moment, he was startled to feel Mia resting her head against his chest. Her arms wrapped around him, and this time her hands rubbed consoling rings on his back.

They just stood that way for a long time, supporting each other.

Thomas wasn't sure how much time had passed when Mia whispered, "Does it ever get any easier?"

Shaking his head, he replied, "I don't know. You learn to live with the hurt. All I know is death isn't the answer to stop the pain."

She looked up at him then, as if she was searching him for something. Sincerity, he supposed. At length, she laid her head on his chest again and gave him a squeeze. "Will you help me through this?"

"As much as you let me. I'm here to guard you by my honor. Heart and health alike."

At this, her gaze flew to his face again, and from her questioning expression he could tell his words may not have been well selected. "I mean, I'm ... here for you. My lady."

A little smirk turned up one corner of her mouth, and she patted him on the chest. "Thank you. Sir Fenwrest."

He raised an eyebrow. "How did you know I pledged myself to the High King?"

"I suppose I didn't for sure till just now," she admitted. "But I saw your sword burning with fire, the way you said Sir Terrillian's did. I had never seen that happen before. I know the legends as well as you. I can't believe they are true."

Thomas smiled. "Come here." Gently he led her away from the edge to more sturdy footing, keeping her close. Once he was sure the roof wouldn't collapse under them in this spot if they moved around a little, he said, "Watch."

Taking another step back, he drew the spiritsword, and instantly the blade caught fire, burning brightly in the dark. In its light playing off her face, he could see the wonder in Mia's eyes. Wonder and some other emotion that was hard to place.

Grinning, he swished the sword around, leaving little trails of flame. That is until he saw something in the distance. Little points of light that had nothing to do with the High King's fiery favor. As far away and tiny as they were, he wondered what they could be.

"Mia, is that a city out there?"

He heard her let out a little gasp. "No. From here, that would have to be the Muiruaine Sea."

"So, those are ships," he replied, his stomach roiling. "We have to tell the others."

"Yes," she replied, hollow. "But Thomas. Please, don't tell them ... well ... don't mention what I almost did."

"Never," he said. "So long as you vow to never take a step toward doing it again. Please."

"I promise."

With that, they climbed down the slopes and broken stone paths with great care and reached the camp. Sir Terrillian was the only one still awake and tending the fire. When he saw them coming, he grinned. "Hey you two, have a romantic moonlit stroll?"

Thomas was stricken for words until he felt a gentle pressure on his arm from Mia. "Um, you might want to wake the others."

Terrillian's face instantly slipped into more serious contours. "What's wrong?"

Mia answered before Thomas could. "Admiral Gelccer's fleet is following along the coast. He's probably planning to round the southern tip of the island. They'll intercept us well before we can make it past Lake Kealn and down to Darby Downs."

Rubbing at the scruffy stubble on his chin, Terrillian huffed. "And we can't double back because they're no doubt pursuing us. Do you know a path past the river ahead?"

"Past the Feathering?" she asked rhetorically. "No. There aren't any good places to ford it, and the only bridges over it will take long enough to reach that they'll still outflank us."

Closing his eyes, Terrillian whispered under his breath, "Great King help us."

When he opened them, he said, "What about the following the Feathering to its end?"

"That's the Imeremare Channel," Thomas noted. "I'm not sure any of us are fit to make the crossing to Libertias by swimming right now."

"Speak for yourself," Terrillian countered with just a faint note of jest. "It sounds like we don't have any better options left. Maybe there will be some small boats from the river there to help us get part of the way across before we have to swim."

Thomas and Mia shot each other a look that confirmed neither held any real hope of that.

"Whatever our lot," Terrillian spoke up again. "We'll wait till morning to wake the others. There's no point in going off into the mountains in this dark. Especially not alongside a mountain river's banks. You two get some sleep. First light, we'll head out."

Mia and Thomas each assented and started off to bed. Terrillian grabbed Thomas's good arm and stopped him. "Sir Thomas," he began, with emphasis on the first bit. "Petition the High King at every juncture possible. We'll need his favor to have any hope of surviving this."

"Yes, Sir Terrillian," he replied, and finding the tree he had claimed, he braced himself against it, closed his eyes, and drifted off to sleep, his repeated pleas for aid on his lips.

18

The sound of the river coursing within its bank beside them being cut by the cries of gulls was as soothing a sound as Thomas could hope for right now. He could taste the building saltiness on the air and knew soon they would leave behind the coastal tree cover and reach the eastern shore.

At his side, Mia stirred and seemed to reach the same conclusion. She leaned her head against his chest. Ever since they left camp at Old Emeral, they had traveled this way. Leaning on each other for support, for strength. Neither wanted to admit how dire their straits were, and neither would let the other give up if they did. It was more than Thomas could have hoped for, given the circumstances.

At the lead was Sir Terrillian. Once Mia had let them all know they could follow the river to the coast, he had taken the front and sometimes strayed ahead by a mile or more from everyone else. He was the group's self-appointed protector and scout. The contrast was stark between him and the other soldiers left. One had deserted after hearing their plight. The others just kept up a glum rearguard, perhaps weighing their chances of escaping if they flew as well.

Gregor kept his own glum march up, and the only time Mia and Thomas would separate was for one of them to take some time walking beside him. He had been given to fits of crying and declarations that he would stay behind and let them take him, because who would hurt a child? Neither had reminded him that Delia had apparently had no qualms with poisoning him herself. Even so, he was on a knife's edge between panic and pushing on.

Of notable calm was the Viceroy, who seemed to have taken this all in stride. A day into their new course, Thomas had learned the Viceroy himself was a Knight of Light, having joined the Order amidst the devastation at Ordumair. Apparently, the same Cinaed who mentored Terrillian had won the Viceroy to the High King's side even as monsters he hadn't intended to unleash turned their fangs on him for his trouble. That was something Thomas often heard the Viceroy reminding himself. "Though trouble come, the good course, the right course, is not altered. It is a hard road, and its reward is ahead, with only a glimpse in hand. And that is enough for the moment. Enough for the moment."

Thomas glanced back at the Viceroy, wondering if he even now were murmuring such to himself. The lean nobleman did seem deep in thought, but his lips were still almost in a pout, and Thomas could see how worn he looked in his smudged finery with his stringy brown hair in disarray. He, too, was starting to look scruffy after this many days on the trek.

"Hey, pay attention," Mia said, tugging at his arm around her.

"Huh?" He peered ahead and immediately made out what she noticed. Terrillian was stopped right at the edge of the trees, before which stretched a very truncated patch of swaying grasses and then the grey waters of the Imeremare Channel. More than that, he could see the two ships anchored at the coast. This was it. If those ships belonged to Admiral Gelccer's fleet, this was the end.

Thomas squeezed Mia's hand that had tightened its grip on his arm. "You with me to the end?"

"Looks like it," she said with a bit of wistfulness. "We won't make it easy for them, will we?"

"Not a chance."

"*Shh*," Terrillian shushed as they came up beside him at the forest edge. "You two can simmer down. Those boats are ours. They're flying the flags of the Commonwealth. I'm not sure how to signal to them, though, and I don't want to risk us going out there without some way of showing it's us lest they unload a few volleys onto the shore."

"A shame we do not have a banner," the Viceroy commented quietly.

Thomas looked down at Mia's dress and then at her and knew they had the idea at the same instant. "Maybe we do," he said. "The colors, at least."

Being careful to cut away only the outer layer of green and gold fabric, Thomas unrolled the makeshift flag and handed one end to Terrillian. "Shall we?"

Bearing his familiar grin, Terrillian nodded. "Let's go.

"Everyone else, try to stay close to the trees. But go ahead and come on out a bit. It may help for them to see a woman in our group, and they might be more trusting if it looks like we aren't hiding anything."

With that, they trotted out onto the beach and, though they could scarcely hope to be heard at this distance, began shouting as they emphatically waved the green and gold sheet along the water's foaming edge.

To Thomas's dismay, the shore wasn't soft sand like some

other spots but rather covered in shell fragments that just kept from cutting into his feet through his overworn shoes. Back and forth, they ran and yelled until, at last, they saw row boats being lowered and heading their way.

Once the boats were a dozen feet from the shore, Terrillian motioned for the others to join them. By then, it was clear that Captain Nerebold was among them. But what made Thomas's heart leap was the sight of the old stern face of Sir Hurstwell in the second boat to drive ashore.

It took everything in him not to run like a child or even a puppy and wrap him in an embrace. From the gleam of a tear in his eye as he came across the sand to them, he was having to contain himself as well.

Captain Nerebold spoke up first, "You all look terrible."

"Hale morning to you too, Arnauld," Terrillian retorted with a laugh.

The captain shot Terrillian a look that was a mix of reprimand and some genuine amusement. "I had thought Hurstwell here a madman when he said you could get this group out of Merlais in one piece. It appears as if the stories out of the North about you and the others were true, Sir Terrillian."

Noticeably, the former privateer did not make eye contact with the Viceroy, even when the nobleman spoke up. "He indeed has been a splendid help in our trials. It seems Black River in Libertias forges formidable patrons of honor and courage."

"Hm. Where's the rest of your party?" Captain Nerebold replied, scanning the trees well behind them. "We have enough room for all of you on these boats, but I'm not sure how many we can get on board before we have to weigh anchor. The Admiral's ships divided to try to trap us in the Channel, and we only have a few hours if we hope to outsail them past the Fell Inlet's entrance. And I daresay we will have scarce enough provisions to make it round the Tislatnean Sea to the Isle of Fens or Albaron."

No one from the group spoke. Hurstwell was the one to break the news, perceiving the silence's meaning. "This is all that's survived the coup," he said with a sigh.

Nerebold's eyes widened, and he gaped. "This is all? They need a hundred times this many to hold the north. At least thirty if they want to make it through the month."

"No, our plight is worse than that," the Viceroy said, his voice steady and authoritative once more. Though his wound had to vex him, he drew himself to his full height. "None of you were privy to the information I received shortly before the coup. But our campaign in the north is already faltering."

"What?" Hurstwell blurted out, stunned as Thomas had ever seen him. "What of the Albarons? And those stoneheads— er, I mean Ords." He shot Terrillian an apologetic look.

"We have been dealt a difficult hand," Ecthelion began, still speaking with calm and an air of authority. "A pestilence has broken out amongst the Albarons and found its way to Ordumair. Though the former is weathering it, their reinforcements will be diminished and delayed at best. The latter is being devastated by the illness and internal strife."

"What do you mean, Viceroy?" Terrillian said, his voice sounding choked.

Sighing, the Viceroy placed a hand on Terrillian's back. "I had hoped to spare you this most of all. Perhaps it is from so many years of isolation, but the Ords are suffering greatly. There have been many deaths and many more gravely ill. It's made their recovery from the siege that much more difficult and has allowed the same faction under Elder Tengrath that almost overthrew the Thane the first time to resurge. I'm concerned they are near a civil war and in as much need of aid as we."

"Send me to them," Terrillian said, his lip quivering from anger or anguish, Thomas could not tell. "If the Thane needs aid, send me. I will remind them that they wisely struck down Tengrath's folly."

Breaking from his courtly manner for just a moment, the Viceroy shrugged. "We can scarce afford to lose you, Sir Terrillian. But if that is where your heart is set, I give you my blessing to ride north."

"We won't be riding north from anywhere if we stand here much longer," Nerebold retorted.

"Indeed," the Viceroy agreed. "Captain, I have asked much of you during this campaign in its best hours. Now in its worst, I have one final request. Deliver me and the others to Tenchford in Libertias, and I will release you from your duty to me. You may keep the ship and all its weapons and cargo as your own to do with as you see fit.

"I know this does not repay the damages you incurred when I criminalized your privateering efforts for Ecthelowall years ago. But it is all I have to offer you."

The scruffy-balding seaman just huffed. "Your offer is well and fine, but you aren't the one I vowed my aid to, Viceroy. I pledged my service to Ecthelowall and did so on behalf of Sir Cinaed and Sir Glewdyn of Black River. Honorable men," he glanced at Terrillian and gave a nod, "I would not turn back on my word to them for all the riches of the Lowlands. So if you're done with your proclamations of doom and pity, I'll be having you all aboard with all haste."

"Wait, Captain," Hurstwell spoke up. "If I may suggest one amendment to the Viceroy's plans."

Sneering and rubbing his forearms with anxious energy and revealing the tattoo of a serpentine dragon on his arm in the process, Nerebold replied, "Fine. Out with it."

"Viceroy," Hurstwell began. "Our enemies know two ships

made it out of Merlais the other night. They also know you escaped with the young ones. Lord Gregor and Lady Mia will be targets of theirs for sure, but you are by far their prize. What if we were to divide the ships? Send me back northward to round the Tislatnean Sea while you and Captain Nerebold thread the Fell Inlet. I presume from there your goal is to seek aid from Libertias?"

"It is," the Viceroy replied, looking very much like a man evaluating the scales at an exchange.

"Good. Sir Terrillian can escort you and your guard as far as Kirke. He is a native, after all. From there, he can ride to Ordumair and I wish him the best."

"That does hold hope of improving our chances," the Viceroy admitted. "Any dissent?"

"I dissent," Thomas said crossly. "If they catch sight of you sailing the flagship back northward, the Loyalists will be sure to sink or swarm you. I can't let you go on a quest like that alone."

"And I cannot allow Thomas to risk his life in such a manner alone," Mia proclaimed, coming to stand next to him.

Thomas almost laughed at how high Hurstwell's brows raised at Mia. "I do not think either of you is suited to—"

"Take them both and take the boy, Gregor," Nerebold said. "We should split our fortunes evenly. The two noble children represent the heirs to Ecthelowall and Emeral, respectively. The Viceroy represents the hopes of the Commonwealth. If we lose one hope then we have the other. Our men in the north will rally just as readily behind one as the other after having seen how ruthless Maldes can be."

"What does that say about our people?" Hurstwell said as he climbed back into one of the boats.

"That this is our most desperate hour," Viceroy Ecthelion replied. "And our people have never faced such a test in the sixteen hundred years since our nation's founding."

"I don't like this," Gregor complained for perhaps the thirtieth time since the ships parted ways. "Why couldn't I go with the Viceroy and a proper ship captain?"

"Cuchulain is a worthy captain of our vessel," Hurstwell replied gruffly. Even his usual even temperament was fracturing. "Ask again and I'll put you in the hold."

The boy scowled back at him. "I'm not cargo."

"Actually, he's right," Thomas said as he joined them on the docks, dropping the hefty load he carried. Terrillian's armor clanked as he did so. He still couldn't believe the other Knight had insisted he take it. "You keep forgetting you're the only legitimate heir to the Monarch's throne. So, you are indeed the Cutlass's most valuable cargo."

"I would give that honor over to you without regret," he retorted petulantly. "And I still don't understand why we cannot make port at Yerst Castle. It is designed to be a haven from enemies."

"Yerst Castle is ancient and not built to withstand the siege engines of our day," Hurstwell stated, pinching the bridge of his nose. "If we make port there Maldes's forces would converge on it and raze the castle. It's safer for us to gather enough supplies here in Kinsbane and keep deep in the Tislatnean Sea till we reach the north."

"Does Kinsbane even have the supplies we need? I thought no one ever travels here. It is on the Isle of Geists, after all."

"Those are just rumors and tales to scare children around fires," Mia reassured him. Dropping off her own load, she stood beside Thomas, leaning against the stacked barrels and bags. Though she tried hard to look at ease and to sound it when talking to Gregor, Thomas knew her nerves were wearing thin. Truth be told, none of them knew what to expect from Kinsbane.

All around, the other crewmates loaded the supplies they had acquired from the locals onto the ship. They were more than half finished now.

"We'll know soon enough," Thomas said. "Once we set sail, you'll have plenty of time to count our stores and remind us of what a bad idea this has been." He took Mia's hand and gave it a reassuring squeeze.

She smiled back thinly. "It's good we have Hurstwell's wisdom and your sarcasm to keep us—"

"Ships on the horizon!" One of the sailors yelled. Running from his post to join the rest of the group, spyglass in hand, he said, "I just got the signal from the ship. They're coming."

"How many?" Hurstwell asked, peering with his hand over his eyes in search of the danger.

"Knowing Admiral Gelccer, there will be at least one frigate and likely two smaller ships, maybe galleys," Cuchulain replied as he helped load a rowboat with supplies.

"They're too small to make out from here," the sailor confirmed. "We'll have to get back to the Cutlass to confirm it's Admiral Gelccer's patrol."

"We need to set sail immediately!" Gregor wailed.

"At the rate they're coming, we won't make it far," Cuchulain countered, twisting the curls of his bushy brown beard around his fingers. "We'll weigh anchor and try to sail straight for Yerst. It wouldn't survive a siege, but the castle should be enough to turn back a patrol. You four should stay here. Captain Nerebold will need to stop here for supplies when he attempts to rejoin us."

"A bold course for you, Master shipman," Hurstwell concluded. "May the High King guard your paths."

The seaman fussed with the amber on his arm bracelet for just a moment and then called out, "All crew to the boats. We're rowing back to the Cutlass and must get underway, now!"

As the crew rushed to do so, Hurstwell commented, "We need to get away from the coastline till the ships pass. Follow me to the trading hovel. We'll get a map from there of the island interior and lay low till the ships pass."

Within minutes the crew of the Cutlass that had come ashore at Kinsbane were back on their ship and getting ready to sail. "We should go," Thomas commented, noticing how Gregor wrung his hands as he watched the ship preparing to sail away. "No need to see this."

"Aye," Hurstwell agreed. "This way." He gestured toward the largest building on the island and navigated around the supplies left behind in the sailors' haste to reach the ship again.

Before any of them could make it five steps toward the trading post, one of the ten residents of Kinsbane ran over to them. "No, no. You must not go into the island's interior. Thelxipeia will not approve so many. You will all be certain to die!"

"Die?" Gregor parroted. "Did I not say this was a wretched mistake?"

"Shh!" Mia hushed.

"Forgive us, sir," Hurstwell replied calmly, careful not to get too close to the man, whose eyes were wild with terror. "We are not familiar with Thelxipeia. Can you tell us why she would wish to slay us?"

"She said only one may approach her directly each year. They must be pure of heart and intent, or they and all the souls on this island will perish."

Hurstwell shot a look at Mia and Thomas, but neither seemed to know what this was about.

Taking care to keep his tone even and soothing, Hurstwell pressed. "Those are strange pronouncements. Perhaps we would understand better if you could tell us more about this Thelxipeia?"

The man looked wary. "You should leave this place. Leave!"

Hurstwell pointed to the Cutlass, which would soon be under way. "I'm sorry, friend. We cannot leave, and being openly among you is too dangerous for you."

The man seemed to understand and said with a huff, "The oracle said if we do not bring her offerings, we die. If we bring too many adorers to her, they die. If we tell others from whence she came, we shall die."

"An oracle?" Thomas mumbled, looking at Mia. She just shook her head.

Hurstwell rubbed his chin. "Very well. I shall take the greatest care with her."

A sudden shift to hopefulness flashed across the local's face. "Will you take her our offering? If you are going to die, it would save us our trouble. And our lives. She sometimes takes those with the offering for her own. Even if they did not seek the secrets of the future."

"No," Hurstwell replied emphatically. "We cannot do such a thing. It is forbidden by the High King's law."

At this, the man burst into hysterical laughter and wandered from them, his path confused and meandering. Every few steps, he would look back over his shoulder and start a fresh fit of hysterics.

Thinking the man a lark, Hurstwell spoke with two other islanders. Each as crazy if not more so than the first.

"I don't like this," Hurstwell whispered to Thomas while Mia got Gregor a bit of hardtack out of their travel pouch.

"And yet, I fear we have no choice. In fact, I can feel the pull of the Great King. This was no coincidental landing. The evil here must be ended."

"Should we leave Mia and Gregor behind for their safety?" Thomas asked, looking at them both. Mia was making a silly face, likely to soothe Gregor's already frayed nerves.

"No. It wouldn't be safe. Do you know how oracles were born in Tislatna?"

"No," Thomas admitted. "I'm not much of a scholar of the Lost Lands."

"They would take a young virgin, usually at the cusp of marriageable age, and offer her in a cultic ritual to goblins."

Thomas's nose crinkled. "Goblins? You mean dark elves? The things parents make up in stories to scare naughty children out of sloth and vice?"

Hurstwell's face was stern and his tone ominous. "I mean cruel and dangerous creatures fallen from their fealty to the High King. They seek the ruin of every man and woman in the Lowlands."

"Do you really believe that these people did that to a young woman here?"

Partially drawing his spiritsword out of its scabbard, the

visible portion of the blade glowed white hot. "I have no doubts about it, Thomas."

Once more, Thomas peered over at Mia and Gregor, a stab of anxiety striking through his core. "How do we proceed then? What do I tell them?"

"I'll get the map. You three stay here. We will tell them what we must as we must. They are not Knights of Light as we are, Thomas. If stories I've heard be true, the High King's light will guard us, but they face great peril if we aren't careful."

Thomas drew in a steadying breath. Whatever Hurstwell's convictions about not scaring them, Thomas owed it to Mia to be honest with her after the night at Old Emeral. They didn't have a lot left now other than each other and the truth.

He waited until Hurstwell had entered the trading post again. With halting steps, he made his way over and cleared his throat. "Mia, can I speak with you a moment?"

"Of course," she replied, puzzled. She must have noticed the discomfort thick in his voice. "You, keep searching in the crates," she instructed Gregor. "There has to be something better to eat than the hardtack that they left."

Striding over to join him several paces away from the boy, she asked, "What's wrong?"

"We might be in trouble," Thomas began. "You heard the crazy man?"

"I tried not to, but he was a bit loud. Why?"

Dropping his voice lower to a whisper, Thomas answered, "Hurstwell thinks the man wasn't crazy. He believes there is a Tislatnean oracle on the island. We could all be walking into a very dangerous situation."

Mia seemed to be sorting something out. After a moment, she chuckled, but there was soberness to her expression instead of mirth. "You know, before you started swinging a sword around that catches fire, I wouldn't have believed that possible."

"But now?"

"But now, I believe you." She put her hand gently on one of the pauldrons he wore, her finger tracing the engravings which glowed like coals.

"Well, I don't," Gregor interrupted. "You must think me a total idiot to start talking about oracles and the like. Do you even know what they say about oracles in the myths?"

"Not really," Thomas admitted. "I couldn't finish proper schooling after my parents died."

He felt Mia slip her hand into his gauntleted one and squeeze it. "Me either. The only thing apart from court etiquette and politics father let me study is botany. And that for practical purposes. A noblewoman like me must have a hobby after all." She said it with slight annoyance.

"And it reminded you of your mother," Thomas murmured, remembering catching glimpses of Mia entranced by the wild flora along the secret paths her mother had shown her.

Mia gave a slight inclination of her head. "I suppose Delia was right about that much. Father had a way of turning what you loved into a prison."

"Stop whispering, you two," Gregor protested. "I preferred it when you didn't fancy each other."

Thomas's felt his cheeks warm and stepped back away from Mia. "Right, well then, give us something worth hearing. What of these myths is so hard to believe after what you've seen and experienced?"

"I have seen precious little beyond your flirting," Gregor said, a cruel smile twisting up the corner of his mouth.

"Don't be a beast," Mia said. "Thomas and I just understand one another."

As Thomas locked eyes with her, he wondered if that really was all that was between them. The gaze lingered and Mia flushed rose. She prompted quickly, "So what do you know of worth—if anything at all?"

"I know plenty. Like to create an oracle, a goblin enters inside the offered one, and they start to become one with its dragonish nature!"

The way he said it was clear he thought this would spook them. But Thomas just raised an eyebrow. "'Dragonish nature'? What does that even mean?"

"It means that what you three gossip and prattle about like nursery runts may be the death of us all," Hurstwell said with a grumble.

Thomas and the others took a start and spun around to face the old soldier. He gave a reproving look to Thomas. "I had hoped to spare you that dread, but it appears prudence isn't something any of you carry in abundance. Now, follow me. We have a trek to make, and I think I found a place for us to stay to wait this out without facing the heart of this isle's dark."

Sir Hurstwell hadn't been purely poetic with his reference to the island's dark heart. It was a steely, overcast day and evening as they trekked up the island's winding paths, hardly as well cut as a deer trail. The island was comprised of large black rocks with strange, wiry trees and scrubby brush. A constant wind buffeted them, sometimes pushing them back, sometimes drawing them up. Always it howled, not loud enough to deafen, but just loud enough to never accord a moment's peace.

Deeper into the island, the stench of a swamp far fouler than the fens on Thomas's home isle was carried to them. There was something unnatural about this place. There was no soothing away the gooseflesh on his arms, though he was sure the armor he wore with its continuous burn was offsetting the effect.

Mia stayed near to Thomas, a thick, simple grey-blue cloak wrapped tight around her. Close on her heels was Gregor, who mumbled and whined about the sights and smells and silliness of it all. Hurstwell seemed the least affected of the group. Or perhaps the most, because he did not utter word. Did not look back, but only followed the map he'd bought.

Drifting nearer still to the putrid swamps, Hurstwell called out, "Here it is. Come on, this is the spot I mentioned earlier." He gestured towards a small cave cut into the hill nearest them.

Recessed into an already-ominous tract of the slope to the island's summit, the dark, foreboding cavern would be enough to give anyone pause. Gregor was beside himself. "That is precisely the sort of cave where bears and all manner of vicious and poisonous beasts reside. I refuse to walk blindly into such a death trap."

"It's not a death trap," Thomas replied, strain evident in his voice. "Besides, it's well concealed and blends into the landscape, so even if someone looks in the area, they're likely to miss it. You're far more likely to die by—"

"By what? Your nonsense bogeys out of a storybook?" Gregor interrupted, overly loud. "I think you vacated the right to speak about what does and does not make logical sense when you embraced that lunacy!"

"Quiet!" Hurstwell insisted. "I hear something."

Thomas strained to hear the sound and found that he could make out a raspy hiss. It grew in volume and began to dip and raise in pitch.

"What is that?" Mia asked. "It sounds almost sweet, but it chills my blood."

"Chills your blood? It is the most beautiful song I've ever heard," Gregor insisted. "We have to find its source. There must be civilized people to have such exquisite music."

The boy tried to head toward the noise but caught a stiff arm across his chest from Hurstwell. "Stop," he ordered. "I have a dreadful feeling about these sounds."

"That's all nonsense," Gregor insisted and slipped the big

man's grasp. He took off at a dash, slipping between trees and scrambling up the rocks to disappear into a fog bank and out of sight.

Hurstwell gaped at the two teens left with him. The look morphed from shock and concern to fury and, with what sounded like a bear's growl, he took off after Gregor.

Mia started after him and Thomas came out of his own stupor long enough to grab her by the wrist and hold her back, "Wait. Something tells me this is the very sort of danger we're meant to guard you from. You have to stay here."

Mia jerked her arm free. "And you have to be crazy. You think I'm safest alone in some dark cave on a cursed island populated by raving madmen?"

A dry chuckle was what escaped Thomas's mouth, but he was much more frustrated than amused. "You're right, it's not ideal. All I can tell you is that in the short time I've been a Knight, I've never felt the draw to unsheathe my spiritsword so potent before. It's like a magnet drawing my hand to it. That means something truly evil is ahead. I refuse to allow it to take you and Gregor."

"I don't suppose I could persuade you by saying I refuse to let such evil harm you either?"

"No," he said flatly and opened his mouth to say something further when Mia put a hand to his lips.

"I tried," she said softly and turned and bolted into the fog.

You are kidding me.

Charging after them all, Thomas felt an icy chill enclose him as he entered the fog. It besieged him, working to find its way past his plate mail to freeze his muscles, his bones, his heart. All the while, the cloying sound of the song grew louder, more intense. No longer resisting, he drew his spiritsword, and immediately it blazed with a righteous fury. The fog's wispy tendrils recoiled from it and he plowed forward as the ground became increasingly sloped downward and soft. "Mia?" he called. "Mia?"

No answer.

"Gregor?" he tried next.

Again, no responses came at first except what he took to be the distorted echoes of his calls, though they sounded curiously feminine. He tried twice more, swiping at the fog with his sword and having no greater fortunes.

His next step faltered as it splashed down into a shallow murky puddle. At least he thought it was a puddle until he took a few more steps and found himself coming out of the fog and faced with a sprawling swamp. At its center was a tree as dark and twisted as any he had ever seen, which bore peculiar green blossoms. Standing some yards back from it were Hurstwell, who held a wriggling and fussing Gregor by the scruff of his tunic, and Mia. She was gazing up at the tree in wonder.

Coming to stand at her side, he huffed. "You're fast."

She didn't respond at first. After a second, she pointed toward the tree. "That shouldn't be here."

"None of us should."

"No," Mia insisted. "That tree—it shouldn't exist anymore. It's a Tislatnean willow. They were all supposed to be destroyed with the island."

The melodic sound from earlier returned, louder. At the four corners of the space, green flames leaped from censers that Thomas hadn't even noticed. Trails of thin smoke twisted from them, creating a strangely aromatic canopy over the otherwise fetid bog.

"Hurstwell, what is going on?" Thomas questioned under his breath.

"Indeed, what is going on?" a distinctly feminine voice

replied and seemed to echo within the space though there were no walls for it to reverberate off of.

Thomas tightened his grip on the spiritsword.

THELXIPEIA

Hurstwell backed up, dragging the still-fussing Gregor with him—closing ranks. He called out, "I am Sir Hurstwell, captain of the guard for Baron Fenwrest of Ecthelowall. We are travelers taking shelter on this isle in the name of Ecthelion, Viceroy of Ecthelowall and the High King of All Realms," he boomed back.

A sound like a hiss cut through the air. "And you presume welcome here under such banners, old Knight?"

"I presume nothing," he shot back, "except that you declare yourself, having heard our declaration. As good form demands."

"Good form? For whom?" The woman said with a derisive laugh. At that moment, the elusive speaker revealed herself. With a swishing gait, she sloshed along about waist deep in the swamp water by the tree. Her hair was in wild tangles, damp as if she had been submerged and perhaps a harvest wheat color when not soaked. By appearance, she was a woman, but young, most likely still in her twenties. She had sharp features, and the dress she wore must have once been silky and elegant.

Presently it was tattered, dirty, and covered in wet algae and moss. Raising both arms, she revealed a sort of draped sleeve that hung off them, reinforcing the sense of the garment's former luxury. She stopped several feet away, water lapping against her torso, and tilted her head as if to demand an answer to her questions.

"The laws of the Viceroy apply to all," Hurstwell replied. "This isle belongs to the Commonwealth, and that makes you its subject."

"You mean this Isle of Geists? Ah, but the Viceroy isn't the ruler of Ecthelowall any longer. Soon enough, he will be no more and all who supported the Commonwealth with him." Her tone was so condescending it almost outcompeted the content of her rebuttal for surprise.

"How would you know that, miss? The isle belongs to Ecthelowall but rarely gets notice or news."

The woman's tongue licked her bottom lip and she looked like she was fighting a fit of gleeful laughter. "Don't you know, Knight? Can't you feel it? Or are your senses dull here? I am Thelxipeia, Oracle of Tislatna Reborn. The one who commands me tells me his plans. You and all your kind are marked for destruction."

Her wicked gaze roved from Hurstwell to Thomas. "Pity you chose to join lot with the fading light in this late hour. We might have had sport with you."

To Gregor and Mia, she said, "You have some promise, young one. And you, girl, have such anger simmering beneath the surface. It would be trivial to bind you both to the shadows. But alas, for you, there is no cause. You are not needed. I will save you for last to savor your terror."

"Save us for last? What is she going on about?" Gregor demanded of the others, at last coming out of the dreamy stupor he'd been in since breaking through the fog.

Now Thelxipeia did laugh, loud and wild and vicious. She rose higher out of the bog. Water streamed off her dress as she revealed her waist and hips and thighs, except instead of showing the delineation of two legs, there was only a horrible singleness. And so, she rose and rose, revealing several feet of musty green- and black-streaked scales. Along the back of which ran sharp barbs the color of darkest night. From the water lifted still more of a whiplike tail covered with the needly spikes.

"She's a ... she's a ..." Gregor stammered.

"She's a monster," Hurstwell finished. He said no words of comfort, drawing his sword and dropping into an aggressive stance. The flames crackled and all but leaped off the blade.

Thomas lifted high the spiritsword entrusted him, glad for the armor Terrillian had gifted him.

The creature narrowed its eyes into slits at the sight of bared spiritswords. It did much to help shore up Thomas's courage. Until now, all he could think about was how big, strong, and deadly this beast-woman looked. His mother had told him stories of rusalka—sirens—which swam the waters around their Isle of Fens and destroyed bad little boys and girls. He had always resented the stories as cruelty. Perhaps they had been genuine warning.

Quick as a viper's strike, the oracle twisted, snapping around her tail's end so that it cracked like a whip at Hurstwell. With surprising speed, he ducked it and shoulder rolled forward. Another twitch of the creature and the tail lashed out at the old Knight. Once more he dodged, but this time he swiped at the tail. Thelxipeia was too quick and a furious back and forth of strikes and misses ensued. Throughout it all, the creature kept making the sounds from earlier, singing—if one could call it that. All Thomas could do was watch with Mia and Gregor in horror and wonder. Any thought of more than that felt hazy, as if steeped in the fog he'd passed through.

Gliding farther out of the bog, the oracle was close enough to bring her pointed tail tip around and force Hurstwell to the edge of the deeper murky waters. Out of them a section of tail swung like a sling shot that had been released. It struck Hurstwell in his breastplate and sent him tumbling down to the water with a groan.

The creature uttered a reptilian hiss of pleasure and tried to wrap her tail around him. Thomas fought the stiffness of his limbs and mental haze. He had to help! She could crush Hurstwell in that common armor. How this occurred to him, he did not know. But he felt sure the Knight armor gifted him by Terrillian and inscribed by the words of the Great King was far hardier.

Just before the loop cinched around him, Hurstwell vaulted over it and, as he spun around, sliced along the side of the tail. Thelxipeia cried out in pain and recoiled, smoke issuing from the wound.

Hurstwell staggered back further into the shallower marshes. He was breathing heavily. Thomas would no doubt hear about the aches from that later.

If there is a later.

The thought had been silent, but the creature's eyes snapped to fix on Thomas. They had grown a poisonous green, and he couldn't shake the feeling that she had somehow heard his unspoken fear and exulted in it.

He could tell she would strike at him now. Shakily, he held up the spiritsword in defense. One bit glowed brighter and he couldn't help noticing the words.

"Fear not, the High King has overcome ..."

Thomas somersaulted out of the way of the first strike. He stumbled and went down hard. There was no time to think;

another snap of the tail was coming at him. With a roll, he let it crash against the small shield he'd been given, and the force of the blow reverberated through him.

What had the Great King overcome? Somehow the answer seemed important.

All at once, he heard a bellow, and Hurstwell was back in the fight. He brought his burning blade around and caught the creature off guard in its fixation on Thomas. It squealed with pain and fury as he sliced off several barbs and inches into its scaly skin.

Thelxipeia pivoted with serpentine finesse to face him and swiped at the old man. He just managed to dodge it.

Thomas started to jump at the oracle, but the moment he raised the sword, those words forced his eyes to them and he had to face them. What had the High King overcome?

Everything. All of the dark. All of the conspiracies and power of the Lowlands. None of it could withstand him.

Wasn't that what he had seen in his vision? The irresistible light; that was the High King.

A rush of warmth engulfed him. His muscles loosened and his limbs grew lighter, his thoughts less fuzzy. Before him, Thelxipeia still loomed enormous and deadly, but his fear seemed no longer a thing that was part of him but a thing he could overcome. A foe to vanquish just like this beast. Life and health were not assured in these Lowlands, but he knew in a way he had not fully faced until now that his aim was the High King's honor, and perhaps that wasn't something that needed his personal victory.

He noticed Mia and Gregor huddling behind a scraggly bush, barely concealed from the terror of it all. Thomas heard the whisper, ever the more familiar and welcome, and he charged, leaping at the monster.

She caught sight of him long before he reached her and

snapped her tail around. But Thomas had known it would come and brought his shield up. It shuddered under the impact and the barbs scraped against its burning surface as it pushed him down into the water with a splash.

Braced for it, the moment he touched solid ground, he slid against the pressure, slipped around and brought his sword down, burning it deeply into the monster's tail.

Were he not in the water, the blow would have severed the tail completely. The blade sank in more than halfway before the creature could recoil. Following up, Sir Hurstwell delivered his own searing blow.

Thelxipeia retreated toward the tree, writhing and pawing at her seething wounds, all the while spewing curses and pleas in alternation.

"Thomas, do you hear that?" Hurstwell wheezed, wiping a bid of mud from his brow.

"Is she speaking in two different voices?" he asked, now that he concentrated.

"Aye."

"Help me!" the feminine voice, absent its echoing quality, called out.

"Grind your filthy carcasses into the meal to whet my hunger," growled another voice, deeper in tone.

Hurstwell motioned to Thomas to draw closer. "The goblin within is losing its hold on the girl. If we can wound it again, I think we can free her."

"Won't that kill her?" Thomas questioned, glancing at Thelxipeia, who was shaking her head as if to clear it. Any moment she might attack them again.

"That's not the nature of the Spiritsword," Hurstwell replied and placed a shaky hand on Thomas's right pauldron. "Now, come around opposite me."

Whether the creature was ready to battle again or not,

Hurstwell charged into the water, hacking side to side as he approached, drawing the creature's attention. At this display, the green villainy returned immediately to her eyes and she hissed, smacking at him with her tail. She connected, but there wasn't as much potency as before.

Thomas worked around to her back, not making a sound more than he could help. He heard Hurstwell grunt as he took another blow but managed to score a glancing hit of his own. Only one second more needed.

The oracle snapped around and surged up, looming over Thomas. She screeched—a terrible, hideous sound—and dove at him.

Thomas was off his footing and slipped, dropping down into the deeper water. Underwater, he knew he couldn't fight her.

Her shadow fell over him before he had to close his eyes from the water lapping over his helmet's visor, and he thrust his spiritsword up, not in desperation, but hope.

Beneath the surface, he felt the blade sink home. Finding the bottom and kicking off, he pushed with all his might, and the blade slid into the creature's hide, deep. Then he was in the air, coughing as Thelxipeia swayed, his sword buried deep in what may have been her abdomen.

In the chaos of her screaming and the smoke pouring from the fiery blade embedded in her, he somehow still heard the whisper instruct him. "Leave her, in the name of the High King!" he bellowed.

The flames surged from the hilt of the spiritsword and blasted the oracle and Thomas apart. Landing in the shallow water, Thomas groaned from the impact but didn't have long to linger on it. His eyes widened as Thelxipeia spewed shadows from her mouth and eyes and every pore. The tail she bore seemed to be part of the shadows and dissipated, leaving a soaking wet and pitiful-looking woman shuddering on the ground.

Over her loomed the coalescing shadow which had the striking green eyes of Thelxipeia's monstrous form. Eyes full of murder and every cruelty imaginable. When the shadows finished coalescing, they settled into a more or less human-like form. Grey-skinned, the features were too sharp, too well matched and striking to be human. A face that would be more handsome to most than bearable, but the moment its eyes fixed on him, it morphed into a hideous beast-like visage so awful words failed Thomas.

Beyond that, the next thing he immediately noted of the creature was its bulk. It was built strongly and had armor of its own. Black armor that was smooth and terminated in sharp edges. A serrated glaive formed in one of its clawed hands. "How dare you," it snarled in the same echoing voice Thelxipeia had, but as much a growl as a hiss. "I was fond of that vessel."

"You'll be fond of the burning abyss soon enough," Hurstwell snapped back, though he was methodically working back around to be closer to Thomas and out of the deeper water.

"Who will send me, you?" The goblin boomed back, the malignant humor from the oracle clearly belonging to it. "What strength do you have left, worm?"

"My prowess is not your greatest concern. Nor is it my truest strength," Hurstwell challenged.

Thomas got beside the older Knight. He could tell now that the barbs had punctured a hole in his armor. There was no telling until the cuirass was removed how badly he had been wounded. From the way he favored that side, though, Thomas knew there was indeed an injury.

"Weak fool. You cannot stop me any more than you can

stop the devastation of your order. The country you served so passionately will be the instrument of ruin for the Lowlands. Even now, the armies of the Dark Prince gather under the guise of Ecthelowall's Monarch. All will be a waste to the ending of the Lowlands."

With a snort, Hurstwell pointed his sword at the goblin. "Certainly not by your hand. You blather too much."

The creature scowled and crossed the distance between them in a single bound. Thomas staggered back as it landed, wondering if it had wings to generate the foul scented wind that buffeted him. It hammered at Hurstwell with its glaive, moving with such speed and ferocious abandon it took Thomas a moment to get a bead on it.

Hurstwell had braced for it, his guards and ripostes ready for each strike. Thomas had never seen him like this. As part of his training, the two had sparred. Never in all those encounters, even those when he felt sure the captain hadn't been holding back, was he anything like this.

He wheeled and ducked and pivoted to strike with a speed and fluidity a master swordsman could only dream of. The flames off his sword encircled him, sometimes warding off attacks singularly. How long could he keep up this furious duel of light against the dark?

Just then, the thing found a weakness in Hurstwell's guard and hammered hard, driving him backward. The elder Knight stumbled and went down onto his back, sword pointed up to ward a finishing blow. It wasn't needed. The goblin was too cruel for that and leaped around, jabbing at him in a playful mockery of his defense.

Suddenly the whisper spoke to Thomas. His grip tightened on the spiritsword in his hand, because Thomas understood. Here was no vague evil of man that is sometimes confused for good. Nor a tortured and animal-like creature like the rusalka.

This was unadulterated evil. A being of darkness standing before him in total rebellion against the High King of All Realms. For all the righteous rage that filled him at the very existence of such a thing, he understood too what was needed of him.

When he dashed, he was a streak. A blur of fire. The goblin scarcely saw the shield before it smashed into its side, sending it tumbling and splashing into the swamp water. Thomas stood over Hurstwell protectively, dropping into a guard stance.

The goblin shook its head and glared at him, baring teeth of unnatural length and sharpness. It barked something he couldn't understand and then charged as it had before, its glaive raised high.

Thomas brought his shield around and intercepted the blow, bearing up under it though the goblin bore down with all its incredible weight and strength. Giving no thought to anything but the strength of the High King to overcome all things, Thomas finally heaved the fiend off.

Immediately he brought his spiritsword around and deflected attack after attack, mimicking Hurstwell in speed and grace and fury. And there was much fury.

Unlike Hurstwell though, he did not seek a line of attack, only holding the creature at bay. Until, at last, it backed away. It did not seem tired, more so vexed. "What folly is this? Do you truly think you can long bear up? You will falter like your mentor, and when you do, you will die a most painful—"

Now Thomas surged forward and jammed his spiritsword forward, forcing the creature on its guard. He pushed off, blocked, ducked, spun and sliced high, then low. Left, right, in quick succession, forcing the creature back.

It seemed utterly startled, but Thomas kept his focus on the whisper guiding each strike. Duck, pivot, parry, riposte. A feint to draw the creature in, he blocked, and then with a deft move, he disarmed the goblin, its glaive landed a smoldering ruin several feet away.

It shook its clawed hand as smoke roiled off it, and it regarded him in a way that now held something else in it. Hatred, not from superiority but fear. "You cannot stop me. You cannot stop anything! You will die, worm!"

Teeth gritted, Thomas gave no reply. He waited, though he was not certain for what.

The goblin shook with rage. "You hear me? You will be a rotting corpse splattered with the blood of everyone you care for!"

When he did not reply, a string of curses again issued from the goblin's mouth that blurred into that language Thomas did not understand. Did not want to understand. The creature was wild with its anger, and it tensed.

Thomas would have thought now was the time to deal a killing strike. Instead, the whisper guided him one step back. To give what seemed a certain advantage. It took all his will to obey, but he took the step back in surrender to the High King. In the next instant, the goblin's clawed hand slashed through the air and buried wrist-deep into the miry soil before Thomas. The foul wind off it ruffled the tunic Thomas wore.

And Thomas knew it was now. Bringing the spiritsword around, he drove it home, deep into the goblin's back, and said, "In the name of the High King of All Realms, whose throne is eternally above all in the Highlands. I command you, begone, be forever banished from the Lowlands."

The flames flared off Thomas's spiritsword and engulfed the goblin. The fiend did not even have the opportunity to cry out in terror, pain, or anger. Blinding light and incomparable heat swelled, and then the foe was gone.

22

Thomas gasped and staggered backward. He stared at where the evil being had been and was no more.

"Hale day, full of such unmerited favor,
Witness to joys and peace as no other,
We celebrate the High King's wonders," Hurstwell recited.

Turning to face him, Thomas rushed over. The old soldier was trying to brace himself up on his elbow and fumbling a bit. Unsure how to help, Thomas lifted clumsily and, between the two of them, managed to get Hurstwell seated up and braced back-to-back with Thomas. "You never told me Knights faced such things," Thomas said at length.

"I never had till now," Hurstwell admitted with a chuckle. "I always wondered how I would fare. Good thing you listen to at least one person."

Cocking his head to the side, Thomas shrugged. "I suppose he is the one to give ear to, if any."

"Who is?" Gregor asked as he stumbled over, muddied and eyes as wide as if he'd had a whole larder full of sugar.

Thomas and Hurstwell each turned to take in the sight, and

153

both burst into laughter. A cathartic expulsion of all the pent-up tension that had built during the battle and before.

"What's so funny?" Gregor asked but chuckled all the same. From beside him, Mia had to join in.

Once the laughter died away several minutes later, Mia spoke up. "We should have listened earlier. If you had told me a month ago—never mind that, three days ago—I'd have seen such a thing, I would have told you a fool drowning in drink has better sense."

Hurstwell groaned and tapped on Thomas to help him to his feet. Thomas obliged but quickly found himself bearing up the older man under the arm. "No harm done, Lady Mia. No one ever wants to believe such evil exists. Nor the good that justly overcomes it." From the way he spoke, it was clear he was clenching his teeth against a sharp pain.

"We need to get you back to Kinsbane and find some medicine," Thomas urged. From the angle he supported Hurstwell, he could see the wound better, and it wasn't something to ignore.

"No, we cannot go back there. The Admiral's ships have to be anchored by now. That's walking into a trap," Hurstwell said with a dismissive shake of his head. "Just help me back to the cave. We'll wait there for dawn and then head to the docks."

"I don't know if it can wait," Thomas insisted.

"And I'm ordering you as your captain and elder to do as I say. Haven't we all learned to obey orders from this?" Hurstwell grumbled, his surly edges enhanced by his pain.

Mia started to speak, but Gregor interrupted, "I'm sorry for running off. I ... I don't know what ..." he trailed off, looking down at the ground, and then wiped away a tear.

Hurstwell grabbed the boy's shoulder and gave him a little shake. "Good. Be sorry. But better than that, learn from it. If what that thing said is true, then there might be a day when you will be asked to lead all Ecthelowall. May the High King help us if you don't learn from today."

"Hurstwell," Thomas reproved.

But Gregor nodded emphatically, "Yes, sir."

"Eh-hem," Mia intoned, shooting Gregor a look. "What about her?"

Thomas strained to see that Mia pointed to the woman, Thelxipeia. She was very still, lying against the roots of the tree that protruded from the swampy water. It was a marvel she hadn't slipped in and drowned. If indeed she was still alive.

Eyeing Hurstwell and then Gregor in turn, he grunted and lifted Hurstwell a little higher, producing a wince and groan from the older man. "Gregor, come here. You can show your penitence by helping our captain."

Hesitantly Gregor slipped into place. When the weight rested on him, he nearly buckled and coughed out, "Oy, yeesh. How many stones is he?"

"Watch it, boy," Hurstwell grumbled. Under better circumstances, he would probably have been amused.

"And don't let him drop," Thomas instructed. Glancing at Mia, he nodded towards the downed woman. "Come on, help me bring her." He took Mia's hand and helped her through the swamp water to the tree. Together, they managed to lift the woman's limp form out of the bog.

The trek to the cave was misery. When they reached it and dropped down inside, all but the unconscious woman were breathing heavily. After a few minutes to recover, Thomas drew his spiritsword to give light. They found the cave was quite deep, but they stayed toward the outside.

After about twenty minutes, they removed Hurstwell's armor and confirmed Thomas's fears about the wound. Using a few offered scraps from Gregor's sleeves, they made a makeshift bandage for it, but that would only do for so long. It was reddening too quickly.

"I should build a fire," Thomas said at length. "Night is on us, and it will be cold."

"No," Hurstwell said faintly. "Don't build a fire. It'll draw attention. Not to mention smoke us out of here. Everyone just huddle for warmth. We only have to make it to sunrise."

Mia shot Thomas a gaze that told him she was as concerned as he that sunrise might be too far off. But Thomas just shrugged and shot her a rueful look. She sighed and tapped Gregor on the shoulder. Gathering around Hurstwell, they all sat propped against the damp cave wall, clinging to one another in silence as night deepened and, with it, the cold. All their hopes were pinned on the morning to come.

23

The tentative fingers of dawn's first foray into the isle's mist-shrouded heights probed into the cavern's opening. They found Thomas only half asleep from cold and an array of discomforts. He sat up, stretching out the aches he had accumulated during the night.

His first thought as alertness came to him again was to check Hurstwell. His breathing was shallow, and sweat beaded his brow despite the cool air. But at least he was alive.

Thelxipeia was still unconscious. Unlike Hurstwell, she never stirred. But for the faint rise and fall of her chest, Thomas would have already given her up for dead.

That's when he noticed Mia sitting near the cave entrance, her green eyes fixed on him. "Hale morning," she whispered.

"Hale morning," he replied. "How long have you been awake?"

"Ever since Gregor elbowed me sometime after midnight," she replied, casting a drowsy glare at the boy who was perhaps the only one of them whose sleep was genuine and deep.

"I won't be missing this cave tonight," Thomas agreed.

"Won't we?"

Moving over to the entrance with her, Thomas dropped down again and was pleased to find that even the faintest touch of the sun's rays was warmer than the cold stones deeper in the cave. "What do you mean?"

"How will we know it's truly safe? Shouldn't we stay here as long as we can help?"

It only took Thomas one glance at Hurstwell to know that wouldn't be possible. "If we don't try, he'll die," he said frankly, remembering the honesty they promised each other.

In the pale morning light, Thomas could see the conflict simmering within Mia. She was looking at Hurstwell as if willing him to be better. "Fine," she said at last with a sigh. "We'll all go down to Kinsbane in a few hours."

Thomas shook his head. "No. You and Gregor should stay here. That way, if the Monarchists are still here, you'll both be safe."

"No, you're not going alone. I'll come at least. Gregor can tend to Sir Hurstwell."

Thomas tried not to, but he chuckled. "No offense to Gregor because he is only a few years younger than us, but if something happens to both of us, he's done for. There's no way he can make it on his own. Or care for Hurstwell, for that matter."

Mia gnawed on her lower lip and huffed. "Fine, then all three of us go. There's little we can do for Hurstwell at the moment anyway."

"That's not happening. Didn't what happened in the bog prove you should listen to me?"

"And didn't what happened yesterday prove none of us should face the danger we're in alone? You've risked enough for us. Or does being a Knight of Light mean you have to die for us?"

There was anger in her voice but pleading in her eyes. Thomas didn't know what to say at first. He hadn't seen it as a compulsion to risk, but their options were few and if anyone had to risk themselves, it should be him. It had to be.

Rising to his feet, Thomas brushed the bits of rock and dirt clinging to him off. "My lady, I have to—"

"Don't do that. Don't try to act like we are different now. I'm not a Lady-to-be any more than you are Baron-to-be." Getting up, she walked over and grabbed his hands. "Don't pretend like we don't know each other. Not after all we've been through."

He squeezed her hands. "Okay, Mia. Then please understand that it is because I know you that I care the way I do. I will not let harm come to you if I can help it."

For some strange reason, he stroked her cheek and brushed some bits of debris from her hair. The look she wore in response was startled at first but then settled into something else Thomas couldn't define.

Mia leaned forward on her toes and kissed him. Not on the cheek or forehead but on the lips.

She pulled away before he could process what had just happened, her eyes just as wide as his. "Um," Thomas stuttered.

"Sorry," she said, her cheeks the same shade as her hair. "I don't know what came over me."

Thomas's brows furrowed for a moment, and he replied, "No, don't apologize. I think you said everything exactly as it needed to be said for us both."

Lifting one of her hands, he kissed the top of her palm. The way her eyes darted to the ground at that moment, he found strangely charming. Thomas had never seen Mia be coy before.

About that time, Hurstwell uttered a low moan and slid

onto the rock-strewn floor. "We're out of time," Thomas said, releasing Mia's hands. "I have to go, now."

"Okay," she said quietly, her gaze intent on Hurstwell.

"I'm leaving the armor. If any soldiers come up here, wear it. It'll keep you protected, and you can use the shield for offense."

"What, no," she said, rubbing her face with a frustrated groan. "Ugh. You need it if you're going to face danger. Besides, it only works for Knights."

"I wasn't one when Terrillian gave me a Spiritsword." Thomas pointed out with a smirk.

Mia crossed her arms over her chest. "Fine."

Turning as if to walk past her, he paused a moment and added. "I have to come back. I want to find out where that kiss leads next."

She gave him a shove. "Oh, get on already!"

Grinning, he took off at a jog, winding his way down the hillside and along the trails until he came to the well-demarcated path along a ridge overlooking Kinsbane. Dropping to a crouch, he tried to keep to cover as he peered out onto the village. There was an eerie calm. No one stirred, and there was no sign of any ships.

Waiting for a few moments longer just to be sure, he smiled to himself and ran down the twisting path into the little sea village. Immediately he regretted it.

Entering the village's makeshift square, he could see a man sprawled on the ground in front of a nearby shop. Thomas swallowed back his anxiety, quickly checked around him, and walked over.

Face down on grey gravel and rocks was the crazy man. Though Thomas regretted calling him such, because he had been right about the danger. Crouching, the teen examined the man for any signs of life. What he found was a wound that had bled freely several hours ago, caused by a rifle shot from close distance. Thomas rubbed the fabric of the man's tunic between his fingers. It was lightly damp, meaning he had been out like this all night.

Standing up and running a hand through his hair, Thomas surveyed the scene. He wished he hadn't. Here in the village, he could see several others lying out in the open. Thomas walked to another, an older woman. By appearances, a rapier had finished her.

One by one, he checked them all until he knew for certain. They were dead, gunshot and rapier wounds staining them scarlet that deepened into maroon.

Thomas drew in a shaky breath. What sort of villain would do such a thing?

Desperate for some hope amid the desolate scene, he ran from one house and shop to another. There were no holdouts hiding within any of the buildings. The chilly wind of the island buffeted him and he shivered. There was no left alive on the island but them.

"The Isle of Geists," he reminded himself without mirth. "It has earned its name ..." Suddenly, a terrible thought seized him. What if the Monarchists had done this and had fanned out across the island? They could be bearing down on Mia and the others. He had to get back now!

24

Thomas sprinted up the slope to the cave and breathed a sigh of relief. Mia and Gregor were sitting outside of the cave in the afternoon sun. To Thomas's surprise, Gregor was twisting Hurstwell's spiritsword around, spinning it point down in the rocky soil. Occasionally shooting a glance over at Thelxipeia, whom they must have drug out of the cave to lay.

"Mia!" he called out once close enough.

Her face brightened, and she was on her feet before two full seconds could elapse. Running at him, Thomas helped close the gap, sucking in much-needed air as he pushed his legs to make this final sprint. A moment later and he wrapped his arms around Mia in a fierce embrace. "I was afraid I'd lost you," he said.

"I worried the same about you," she replied though there was a tempering to the pleasure in her voice.

When he pulled back, he noticed the redness and puffiness around her eyes. She had been crying. "What's wrong?" Thomas asked.

"Hurstwell didn't make it, Thomas. He passed on while

you were away," she said, her voice low as she gently rubbed at his arms.

Pulling back, Thomas shook his head, "No, he was stronger than that. Check again, he's going to be fine."

Looking around he saw the dark outline of Hurstwell in the cave still. Thomas ran over and dropped to his knees beside the captain. He held his hand over Hurstwell's mouth and felt panic rising in him when no breath brushed his palm. Bending low, he listened for the sound of his heart. There was only silence.

Once more he checked for breath and then a heartbeat. He shook the old soldier. "Come on, you can't give in yet. We're not out of this yet. You can hang on!"

He checked for breathing and a heartbeat one last time and dropped to the floor, head between his knees. Tears wouldn't come, dehydration and fatigue saw to that, but the pain that radiated out from Thomas's core sent shudders through him, and a low moan escaped his lips.

After several minutes passed, he got up, needing to do something. Anything.

He grabbed Terrillian's armor which lay nearby and put it on, its weight and warmth welcome and steadying. When Thomas emerged from the cave, Gregor and Mia were both waiting for him. Thomas couldn't hold Mia's gaze. "He's gone. I failed him."

"It's not your fault," Mia insisted. "You did all you could under terrible circumstances."

"She's right," Gregor piped in. "It's not your fault, it's mine. I'm the one who ran off when he said to stay here. I got him killed." Lips quivering, the tears did come for the younger boy. "I'm so sorry. I didn't mean for this to happen."

"No one ever does," Thomas replied, his voice hard as

stone. Then added gentler, "I don't think Sir Hurstwell blamed you."

"He didn't," Mia confirmed. "Hurstwell woke up some time after you left. It was hard to hear him, but he did say to tell you both it wasn't your fault what happened to him."

"'Evil ends must come till the Lowlands are renewed,' were his words for it," she added. "He gave Gregor his spiritsword, and he wants you to teach him all you know. He said you're the Captain of the Guard now. Long may you guard the land and its lord. Long may the High King's favor be upon you.'"

Thomas drew in a shaky breath. Staring at the entrance to the cavern, Thomas suddenly commented, "I'm going to get some rocks."

One by one, arms quaking from the effort, he hefted the largest stones he could find. After a little while, Mia and Gregor joined in, helping him cover the entrance to the cave. When it was done, Thomas was at a loss for words. Every funerary event he had ever attended had them. His parents had great flowery speeches by many about the splendor of House Fenwrest. Even as a child, he understood those to be artifice. Few, if any, truly knew his father well enough to say such things.

All of a sudden, Gregor spoke up, reciting an old Ecthel eulogy given at funerals for nobility:

"Where shall we find a heart as noble as thine,
Among the towering emerald pines,
You were like the Golden Orchard full bloom,
Bringing to all Ecthelowall hale in gloom.
Just as the golden leaves were burned,
Our loss of you will be ever mourned.
And in the endless ages ahead,
Find the High King's peace and rest."

When Gregor finished, he kicked at the ground and said, "Until now, I always found those words silly nonsense. That must have been because I never knew anyone truly noble before."

Feeling the grief tearing him apart from within, Thomas needed a distraction. He took note of the sun's progress in the sky and knew they needed to be going soon.

"Did Sir Hurstwell say anything else?" Thomas asked, staring at the makeshift tomb.

"Yes. His last words were, 'Do not be afraid ... the High King has overcome and triumphed.'" Mia ventured.

"Those sound like him."

After a few minutes of silence, Mia prompted, "What should we do now?"

"We should head to Kinsbane. We'll need shelter and supplies."

Gregor was standing by the stone heap, staring at it intently. Anxiety lined his chubby face, and he had taken to spinning the spiritsword in front of him again.

"Did the villagers say the Monarchists had already passed by?" Mia asked. "And what will we do with the defeated oracle?"

Rubbing his face with both hands, Thomas tried to keep at bay the revulsion he felt at the memory of what he had found. "They said nothing. None were left alive to speak."

Out of the corner of his eye, Thomas saw Gregor stop spinning the sword and stare at him. Mia's mouth opened, but no words came out. Finally, she pursed her lips and nodded towards Thelxipeia. "We'll need to carry her. We should leave now if we want to make it to the village by sundown."

"Right," Thomas said. "Gregor, you help Mia on her end. It's going to be a difficult trek."

"Not to complain, but are we near Kinsbane yet?" Gregor asked with a groan. "This is a special kind of torment."

The sun was sinking into the sea on the western horizon, setting ablaze the waves with orange and gold and magenta. It seemed strange to Thomas that the world had gone on as usual and could even look lovely. Shaking out of the stupor, he replied, "It's just over the ridge. We can stop here to catch our breath."

"What should we do if she wakes," Mia wondered aloud as they laid Thelxipeia down. "I can understand she wasn't in control of herself. But I can't forget she was the one trying to kill us all. In a way, she killed Sir Hurstwell."

"No, I did," Gregor amended. "It was my fault."

"It wasn't any of our faults," Thomas insisted with quiet firmness. Even so, he couldn't bear looking at Thelxipeia. Mia was right to question what they would do with her. Wandering to the edge of the ridge, Thomas's heart sank. A ship was moored off the coast with one rowboat docked on the island

and another nearing filled with soldiers bearing lanterns and torches.

How were they supposed to escape this? Every bit of him felt exhausted, unable to muster the will to flee. His knees were ready to buckle under the weight of this discovery.

But then Thomas thought of Hurstwell, how he had fought on without letting up when he had to have known the seriousness of his wound. Surely, he could give whatever he had left to save Mia and Gregor. His hand drifted to the hilt of his spiritsword. One final battle to keep them safe, to let them make it safely from this cursed place that would become his burial site as well.

Just then, someone emerged from the storage depot with two others. He seemed to be having a conversation with the other men. They were looking around the village, hunting for them. The party's leader turned and scanned the horizon in Thomas's direction.

Thomas dropped to the ground, his heart pounding in his chest. He had been counting on surprise. Now he did not even have that to aid him.

"Hello there," called out one of the men from below. "A hale evening for the Monarch is a dark one for Ecthelowall."

Though it could be a trap, the words so surprised Thomas that he got back up and found the speaker. The man pulled back a hood on the green cloak he wore, and Thomas almost couldn't believe it. Jumping to his feet again, he called back, "Ahoy there!"

"Are you mad?" Mia asked, trying to jerk him back down.

"It's Captain Nerebold," Thomas explained.

"Truly?" Mia leaped to her feet to get a look herself. By now, Nerebold and his crew were heading up the slopes toward them.

Spinning to face Thomas, Mia grabbed him in a fierce

embrace. He held her back just as tightly. This was it, their moment of rescue, and Hurstwell's last words kept coming back over and over again: *"Evil ends must come till the Lowlands are renewed."* With them were also the words on the spiritsword that had shifted things decisively for him in the battle against the goblin.

As he gently rubbed Mia's back, he said softly, "The High King triumphed over evil. No matter where we go from here. Our hours of desperation are at an end. From this moment forward, we press on in hope."

BONUS CHAPTER

"What do you think?" Cinaed asked, folding the Lyrscony newspaper bearing the date "Gŵylgoleuni 23, 355 Modern Era." He peered up at his host. In the back of his mind, the date on the paper was a solemn reminder they had passed the winter solstice, and time was all the shorter for them.

"What you are proposing is death," the spindly Antoni stated flatly. He looked down from his uplifted aquiline nose with superiority. Graying and wrinkled as he was, Cinaed Black could remember when Antoni was a child. He hadn't been so overbearing then.

Cinaed sighed and tapped his fingers on the oak table he sat beside. "Perhaps I am being rash," he allowed. "But only in my execution. Not in my intentions or assessment of our situation. We must gather the Defenders of the Realms to Council."

Antoni scoffed. "That is a bold assertion. We can scarce

peek out from our holes in the ground without losing our heads, and you want to convene a committee."

Cinaed sighed. "You still feel that way after all you have told me?"

"What, the leader of Rehalcyon's armies being named Maldes Ilyron? You do spook too easily. There's no chance it could be the same Monarch Ilyron as in Ecthelowall's histories."

Once more, Cinaed drummed his fingers on the table, unsure how to respond. He glanced across the room, strewn with books and papers, to the nook where his granddaughter Aria sat. She was twirling strands of her dark hair around a finger, looking out into the encroaching twilight as though oblivious to Cinaed and Antoni's conversation. The old man knew better, however. No doubt Aria heard every word, even if only just through the thick haze of her melancholy.

"Tell me again," Cinaed began. "Your contact in Brackenburgh said he had inquiries from a young man about Aria's age, looking for us?"

Splaying his hands after taking a sip of coffee, Antoni said, "Yes, that is what he told me. The young man claimed to have escaped the Ministry of Justice and was looking for you. Whether for good or ill, I cannot say. Though my contact felt him honorable enough to arrange a meeting with me."

Cocking his head to the side, he asked, "Do you know him?"

Cinaed pursed his lips, considering that question for a moment. "If he is the youth I believe, yes."

"Is he friend or foe?" Antoni asked, leaning forward and lifting a brow.

A clicking rang through the air before Cinaed could respond. Antoni scooted his chair back. "Ah, my apologies. We are receiving a telegraph. Marvel of the modern world. I'll be back in a moment."

As soon as Antoni left the room, Aria drifted over to Cinaed's side. "The group waiting for us outside hasn't left. Is it wise to wait till dark to confront them?"

"It isn't unwise, given what our larger goals are in being here. We need Antoni to contact the Defender of the Southeastern Realm for us. Whatever his protests to the contrary, we must press on with assembling the Council."

Aria nodded quietly, her lips set in a tight line, arms folded at her waist. She didn't say anything else.

"You miss him," Cinaed surmised.

"I—" Aria hesitated. Her green eyes assessed him like a dubious salesman. "Yes. I don't want to talk about it."

"Certainly not," Cinaed agreed and took his granddaughter's hand and kissed it lightly. "For the moment, we need not speak further of Jason. But there will come a time when you will have to face him."

"Not if the three Sombra waiting for us have their way."

He eyed her soft cheeks and graceful brows for signs of genuine concern. The ancient assassins who could merge with the shadows and perform all manners of dark horrors had a score to settle with them. But the only thing Cinaed could discern from Aria's impassive demeanor was how very hard she was trying to avoid mentioning or thinking of Jason. Or so it seemed to his old eyes. Though it was impossible not to think that the Sombra were pursuing them because of the losses they incurred when Cinaed and Aria had rescued Jason from the outskirts of their stronghold.

At the time, he hadn't known that Ilyron was back. The attack had seemed so capricious. Even for a family as twisted and cruel as Jason's, hiring the arcane mercenaries to murder him was extreme. But now the pieces were fitting together.

Surely even Antoni, contented to hide as he was, had to see that.

Cinaed got to his feet, an ache shooting through his back. His long duster drifted aside, revealing the hilt of his spiritsword. He gripped ahold of it briefly, feeling the warmth that coursed through it into him, then covered it again.

"I will let Antoni know we are leaving," he informed Aria.

Her brows knitted. "But how will we find Defender Miguelso without him?"

"I have a few other old friends to seek out. Though we will need to travel to Garcenilles to find them."

She didn't say anything, but from how her face fell, he could tell she understood the change in plans would make it almost impossible for Jason to find them. Presuming he was indeed the young man seeking them out.

"Well, this is interesting," Antoni announced as he re-entered the room, his attention fixed on the scrap of paper he carried. He looked up at the last second before bumping into Cinaed. He eyed the pair curiously and then said, "It appears Defender Kharoum is trying to get word to you. He needs aid and is quite desperate."

Cinaed tried to keep his expression neutral. Sadiq expelled them more than a week ago. It had, in fact, led to Jason rashly running off to Brackenburgh in the first place. "Did he give any indication of the cause for his need?"

"None," Antoni replied. "With him, I would wager comfortably there is some scheme to aid Zilnen against the Empire. Rehalcyon is building up that port city between Zilnen and Surcalido. Rumor has it the navy they're building there will finally break the supply chain from Ecthelowall keeping Zilnen from collapse."

There was no subtle way to ask whether Sadiq had changed his mind about the Council as part of the deal without alerting Antoni to that roadblock. The Lyrsconian had enough reasons to dismiss Cinaed's pleas without adding to them. "We should go to him, all the same. He is a member of the Order in need."

"You need not worry yourself about him," a raspy voice hissed.

In a dark corner of the room, the shadows began to deepen and what looked like black tendrils twisted upwards and together until they formed a darkling man in a hooded cloak and cowl with grey skin. He wore a light suit of black mail over a billowy tunic, and on each forearm wore bands bearing the symbol of Tislatna. Pupilless milky eyes glared at them balefully.

"A Sombra," Antoni murmured, already shrinking backward.

"Yes," the creature replied. "And none of you vermin will be leaving this rathole." As he said this, he produced a long dagger that glinted even in the room's low lighting.

Cinaed pushed back his duster and drew his spiritsword in one smooth movement. As he did, fire caught along the long, broad blade sending a rush of heat up Cinaed's arm. A hazy pall that had come over the room was pushed back as the flames crackled. At his back, he knew Aria had drawn her rapier-like spiritsword as well.

"Aria, you said there were two more. You and Antoni watch for them. I will handle this fiend."

Cinaed's granddaughter nodded and trekked to the door, eyes fixed on the sombra. A moment later she and Antoni were outside. Cinaed tensed his muscles, readying for the fight ahead.

"They told me you are a bold one," the Sombra replied, raising a hairless brow. "Too bold, I say." One of his hands reached into the dark space between his tunic and the cloak. It emerged as a nebulous obsidian mist. With lightning speed, it reformed into a barbed whip and cracked at Cinaed.

There wasn't much room to dodge in the minimalist quarters. Cinaed managed to use the hall to the apartment's bedroom as a shield. The black whip raked across it sending splinters of wood off in a spray.

A close one. Drawing in a deep breath, Cinaed, as he always did, appealed to the High King: "Strengthen and guide me so as to bear well your banner, my Mighty King."

Warmth flooded his limbs, and the voice of the High King was in his ear, guiding him. Whirling out from his hiding place, he brought his spiritsword around and battered aside the Sombra's attempt to stab him with the dagger.

The creature looked duly shocked. He had made no sound, been totally out of sight, and moved faster than humanly possible. Unfortunately for him, it was he who had been too bold.

Before the other could recover, Cinaed brought his sword back up and around, slicing his burning blade across the Sombra's palm.

Collapsing backward in an amorphous cloud mist and screeching in pain, the Sombra reformed several steps away, shaking his smoking hand.

"You need not follow the path you've been on. I can help you find your way out of the darkness."

"And you can die, you old fool," the fiend snarled back, snapping his wrist to send the barbed whip straight at Cinaed's face.

The aged Knight had already been guided to sidestep the strike. And the next which followed and thereafter the final desperate crack just before Cinaed reached the monster and plunged the burning Spiritsword into its gut.

A gasp escaped the Sombra's masked lips, and flames immediately swelled and caught onto the tunic it wore.

Cinaed waited a moment and said again, "It's still not too late."

"Curse you," the Sombra spat, and a moment later in a flash of flame and a sharp crackle, the shadow being was no more.

Cinaed sighed heavily, feeling the weight of what had transpired as he always did. He took in several deliberate breaths and glanced across the space. On the opposite end of the room, the door to the apartment was open. A few moments later, Aria and Antoni returned.

"The other two have retreated," Aria announced. Her eyes drifted to the room's damage and then to her grandfather. "Are you okay?"

"Always."

"The Sombra?"

"He is vanquished," Cinaed replied without relish. To Antoni he addressed, "Do you see now the importance of bringing together the Council? Night has fallen, and we bear the light to see the Lowlands through it."

Antoni licked his lips and produced a handkerchief with which he dabbed the sweat off his forehead. "I suppose I must." He stalked gingerly through the debris of his home and paused before disappearing into his study to turn and say, "Give me a moment to retrieve my materials. But let me just say, you are every bit as stubborn as the New Ecthelowallers who still think Emeral can be independent."

In his absence, Aria spoke up, "He's right, you know. You are as stubborn as the Emeralans from the stories you told me."

Cinaed chuckled throatily, but the humor quickly faded. "Monarch Ilyron figured prominently in those stories. You know how they ended. Whatever Antoni's convictions, we must gather the Council."

"Is that why you plan to help Sadiq even after he banished us and drove Jason away?" Aria asked, thinly masking the hurt and accusation in her tone.

"It is the right thing to do," was all the reply he gave her.

Silence fell between them until, a few minutes later, Antoni returned with a ledger and handed it to Cinaed. "Everything you need to find Defender Miguelso is here. As well as directions to get to a secluded location to assemble the Council," Antoni explained. "It is all I can do, and I'm afraid very soon I will need to disappear for a time."

Placing his big, worn hand on Antoni's shoulder, Cinaed smiled warmly. "This is more than enough. Thank you." He paused, glanced at Aria, and cleared his throat. "Forgive me, though, but I have one further request. The young man your contact in Brackenburgh mentioned. Please, do meet him. Make sure he finds his way to us in Zilnen."

Antoni arched his brow. "He is important then?"

"All who have chosen to follow the High King are a treasure to our Lord. It is our duty as ennobled among his servants to make sure Knights such as he achieve everything the High King intends. His quest, my quest, the Quest. They all intertwine."

"I understand. I will take care of the boy." Antoni's demeanor shifted from solemn to surprised as Cinaed began gathering his effects. "Are you leaving in the middle of the night, Defender?"

"Yes, we need to reach Zilnen by tomorrow evening. These are desperate times, make no mistake. But desperation is an opportunity to see the High King's royal power fully displayed. Hold onto that hope and encourage others to do the same. We're nearing the turn of a new chapter, and none of us can guess what will come next."

ABOUT THE AUTHOR

Brett Armstrong has been exploring other worlds as a writer since age nine. Years later, he still writes, but now invites others along on his excursions. He's shown readers haunting, deep historical fiction (*Destitutio Quod Remissio*), scary-real dystopian sci-fi (*Day Moon and Veiled Sun*), and dark, sweeping epic fantasy (*Quest of Fire*). Every story is a journey of discovery and an attempt to be a brush in the Master Artist's hand. Through dark, despair, light, joy, and everything in between, the end is always meant to leave his fellow literary explorers with wonder and hope. Always busy with a new story, he also enjoys drawing, gardening, and spending time with his wife and son.

You can learn more about Brett by visiting his website: BrettArmstrong.net

MORE FROM THE QUEST OF FIRE SERIES

The Gathering Dark

Quest of Fire Series – Book One

**After a thousand years of light, a teen's world teeters
on the edge of utter darkness.**

On the run from his past, Jason hides in an inn where he hears a tale
from centuries past about Anargen, a teen on a quest to bring peace
between Ecthelowall's men and Ordumair's dwarfs. But an arcane
evil seeks to ruin the peace talks and ensure a lost dwarf treasure isn't
found by those for whom it's meant. As he listens, Jason realizes the
story is more than a fable and he must choose whether to join
Anargen's quest, which has shaped and can destroy his world.

Get your copy here: scrivenings.link/thegatheringdark

Succession: A Novella

Quest of Fire Series – Book Two

The heir must prove his worth - or die trying

Son of the Northern Realm's Defender, raised among the dwarves of Ordumair, Meredoch was anticipated to succeed his father. Some whispered he would bring the longed-for peace between Ordumair and their ancient foe, Ecthelowall. All of that changes when Ordumair's Thane is killed and Meredoch and his family are exiled. From prestige to poverty, the young boy must chart a new course. Battling creatures believed only myths and racing against evil toward the prize, Meredoch must face the truth of his place in the world and claim his right of succession.

Get your copy here: scrivenings.link/succession

Shadows at Nightfall

Quest of Fire - Book Three

The hour has arrived … with all its terrors.

The shadows of Jason's past have caught him. Having stepped into the Quest of Fire, Jason is pursued by a league of assassins formed of pure darkness. To his horror he discovers these creatures were also contracted to eliminate Anargen and his friends as they sought to understand the Tower of Light's oracle. To unravel the mystery of who wants him dead and how he fits into the ages old quest, Jason must travel the lengths of the Lowlands. He'll have to move fast, the darkest creatures in the Lowlands have long waited for this hour. With few concerned for the light and everything falling apart around them, Jason and Anargen will face the shadows of night's falling as their world hangs in the balance.

Get your copy here: https://scrivenings.link/shadowsatnightfall

TOMORROW'S EDGE TRILOGY BY BRETT ARMSTRONG

Day Moon

Tomorrow's Edge Trilogy Book One

Eluding authorities, one teen holds the past and future's key.

AD 2039: Project Alexandria is an initiative to give all humanity safe and equal access to all recorded knowledge. But the prodigious teen Elliott knows something is wrong. There are dark intentions behind Project Alexandria and the key may lie in the last print copy of Shakespeare's complete works that contains a sonnet titled, "Day Moon". Racing along a path made perilous by federal agents and betrayals from those closest to him, Elliott must uncover the sonnet's secrets. All of history past and to be depends on it.

Get your copy here: https://scrivenings.link/daymoon

(Available September 20, 2022.)

Veiled Sun

Tomorrow's Edge Trilogy Book Two

The pieces to rescue the past and future come together.

AD 2040: Every day the world slips further into lies. Seventeen-year-old Elliott knows that better than most. Project Alexandria is rewriting history, shaping the world according to sinister goals. To stop it, Elliott must assemble the "Veiled Sun", a secret program written by his grandfather. The only people he can count on are siegers—outlaws who use their coding skills for purposes almost as nefarious as Project Alexandria. Overcoming the schemes and betrayals all around him, he's the world's best hope to save reality, if he doesn't lose hold of it himself.

Get your copy here: https://scrivenings.link/veiledsun

(Available October 18, 2022.)

RECENT TITLES FROM EXPANSE BOOKS

Beyond the Gates by Erin R. Howard

Gates of Deceit - Book One

If playing by the rules means it keeps you alive, then seventeen-year-old Renna James should know better. She is, after all, the one who broadcasts these rules to the Outpost. What lies beyond the gates had always lured her, but her venture outside wasn't supposed to leave her locked out. Now, Renna's one chance to survive the next seventy-two hours just ran into the forest she's forbidden to enter.

Get your copy here: https://scrivenings.link/beyondthegates

The Girl with Stars in Her Eyes by Dawn Ford

Firebird Series - Book One

Eighteen-year-old servant girl Tambrynn is haunted by more than her unusual silver hair and the star-shaped pupils in her eyes. Her uncontrollable ability to call objects leads the wolves who savagely murdered her mother right to her door.

When she's fired and outcast during a snowstorm, her carriage wrecks and she's forced to find refuge in an abandoned cottage. There, her life is upended when the magpie who's stalked her for ten years transforms into a man, Lucas. He's her Watcher and they're from a different kingdom. His job is to keep her safe from her father, an evil mage, who wants to steal her abilities, turn her into one of his undead beasts, and become immortal himself.

Can they make it to the magical passageway and get to their home kingdom in time for Tambrynn to thwart her father's malicious plans? Or will Tambrynn's unique magic doom them all?

Get your copy here:

https://scrivenings.link/thegirlwithstarsinhereyes

Stay up-to-date on your favorite books and authors with our free e-newsletters.

ExpanseBooks.pub (an imprint of Scrivenings Press LLC)

9 781649 172341